What's a g
finds herself in

*If she's with the right person, the possibilities
can be absolutely mind-blowing!*

Don't miss another sizzling installment
of one of Blaze's most popular miniseries:

24 Hours: Blackout

JUST FOR THE NIGHT
by Tawny Weber
(May)

MINE UNTIL MORNING
by Samantha Hunter
(June)

KEPT IN THE DARK
by Heather MacAllister
(July)

24 Hours: Blackout—
No lights. No power. And no holding back...

Dear Reader,

I hope you're enjoying the 24 Hours: Blackout miniseries so far—*Just For the Night* by Tawny Weber and *Mine Until Morning* by Samantha Hunter.

My contribution to this trilogy, *Kept in the Dark,* is the story of trust and second chances between a former cat burglar and her ex-lover—the security expert who sent her to prison. Talk about conflict!

Although my heroine says she doesn't believe in second chances, there are lots of people who do—including those who run animal shelters. These volunteers see to it that lost and abandoned pets get a second chance for a happily ever after. Check out the Blaze Authors' Pet Project at www.BlazeAuthors.com/blog where we highlight different animal shelters. Who knows? Maybe you'll find a new best friend like the wily Jo Jo, who scampers through *Kept in the Dark.*

Best wishes,

Heather MacAllister
www.HeatherMacAllister.com

Heather MacAllister

KEPT IN THE DARK

Harlequin®

TORONTO NEW YORK LONDON
AMSTERDAM PARIS SYDNEY HAMBURG
STOCKHOLM ATHENS TOKYO MILAN MADRID
PRAGUE WARSAW BUDAPEST AUCKLAND

Recycling programs
for this product may
not exist in your area.

ISBN-13: 978-0-373-79630-4

KEPT IN THE DARK

Copyright © 2011 by Heather W. MacAllister

ABOUT THE AUTHOR

Heather MacAllister lives near the Texas gulf coast where, in spite of the ten-month growing season and plenty of humidity, she can't grow plants. She's a former music teacher who married her high school sweetheart on the 4th of July, so is it any surprise that their two sons turned out to be a couple of firecrackers? Heather has written more than forty romance comedies, which have been translated into twenty-six languages and published in dozens of countries. She's won a Romance Writers of America Golden Heart Award, *RT Book Reviews* awards for best Harlequin Romance and best Harlequin Temptation and is a three-time RITA® Award finalist. When she's not writing stories where life has its quirks, Heather collects vintage costume jewelry, loves fireworks displays, computers that behave and sons who answer their mother's emails. You can visit her at www.HeatherMacAllister.com.

Books by Heather MacAllister

HARLEQUIN BLAZE

To get the inside scoop on Harlequin Blaze and its talented writers, be sure to check out blazeauthors.com.

Don't miss any of our special offers. Write to us at the following address for information on our newest releases.

Harlequin Reader Service
U.S.: 3010 Walden Ave., P.O. Box 1325, Buffalo, NY 14269
Canadian: P.O. Box 609, Fort Erie, Ont. L2A 5X3

To Marilyn, Carla and Barb,
and many more breakfasts at Denny's

1

Brooklyn, New York
Six years ago

"Don't be a fool, Kaia."

Kaia Bennet's father gestured dramatically, his hand crashing into her roommate's study lamp. As he steadied it, Kaia dumped the dirty clothes from her backpack into a mesh hamper sitting on her closet floor. She'd planned to change her T-shirt before class, but not while her parents were in the room.

"I'm not." She inhaled, secretly smiling when she caught Blake's scent mingled with hers. "I'm a student. Just like everyone else."

"You are *not* just like everyone else." He made a sound and muttered, "I thought you would have outgrown this phase by now."

"It's not a phase. It's what normal kids my age do."

One of her bras slid off the mound of dirty clothes to the floor of her tiny dorm room closet. She kicked it out of sight and bent to open the bottom dresser drawer. The drawer wouldn't open all the way unless she moved the bed, but her father was standing on the other side of it, being parental.

Her mother had positioned herself in the doorway where she could keep a lookout.

Typical. What wasn't typical was her parents making a trip into the city to see her.

"How can you live like this?" her father asked, looking around the cramped space.

"She can't. That's why she hasn't been back in three days," her mother snapped.

Her father looked pained. He was very good at looking pained.

Kaia stood upright clutching a sports bra; it was the only clean underwear she'd found in the drawer. "Have you been spying on me?"

"No," her father denied at the same time her mother said, "Yes."

"Louisa, it's not spying to be concerned about our daughter's welfare."

Her mother ignored him. "You haven't checked in with Roy Dean for your messages."

"He goes by Royce now," Kaia reminded them knowing her friend would always be Roy Dean to her parents.

She stuffed the sports bra into her backpack along with her last clean pair of jeans. Actually most of her clothes were in the mesh hamper. Mentally shrugging, Kaia pulled the drawstring on it closed and prepared to take it all with her. She could do her laundry at Blake's. "You know, most parents just call or text their kids when they want to talk with them. They don't message through a go-between."

Most kids didn't have jewel thieves for parents, either.

"We prefer to stay off the grid."

Tell me something I don't know. Kaia met her father's dark gaze squarely. "I don't have any reason to stay off the grid." It was impossible once she'd enrolled at Brooklyn College, anyway. "And I never will again." She added that last bit in case they were here to try to talk her into doing a job with them.

They were getting older, although her mother's hair was still as black as Kaia's without the need for hair dye. But after her mother's long ago fall, Kaia had been the one to climb over roofs, scale buildings and slither through air ducts.

Until she was old enough to say no and move out.

As she returned her laptop and other class materials to her backpack, she was aware of the long look her parents exchanged.

"You fixed for money okay?" her father asked.

"I'm fine." More than fine.

"We heard about the job," her mother said, and quickly glanced up and down the hallway.

"Yeah. It seems I have a knack for selling jewelry. Who knew?"

"We're not talking about your minimum-wage job at the mall." Her father reached across the bed and tapped the tiny lump at her throat.

Rats. She'd hoped they wouldn't notice the necklace beneath her T-shirt.

"Roy Dean mentioned a diamond," he said.

"Royce," she emphasized, "talks too much." Before her father could ask, Kaia tugged on the gold chain so he could see the stone.

He glanced at it and in that brief look, Kaia knew he'd assessed the grade, carat weight and color. Way too puny for him.

"Interesting flaw enhanced by the marquise cut. Like

a cat's eye. A cat's eye for a cat burglar. I see why it appealed to you." He dropped the pendant and moved to the doorway, relieving her mother, who limped over to have a look at the stone, herself.

Kaia rolled her eyes, both at their paranoia and the exaggerated limp.

"I saw that," her father said without looking at her.

Her mother stared at the necklace and then at Kaia. "You didn't get that at your little rinky dink mall jewelry store."

"It was a gift."

"Not from your boyfriend," her mother said sharply.

Kaia shouldn't have been surprised that they knew about Blake. "No."

"Casper Nazario?" asked her father from the doorway.

Kaia gasped. Now they *had* surprised her. "I—"

"Does he know you have it?" her mother interrupted.

"Of course. He *gave* it to me."

Kaia's mother looked toward the doorway and her parents changed places again.

"Payment? For the job?" Her father appeared genuinely concerned.

What was he thinking? "Yes! I mean, no, he paid me money for the job. This was something else. A bonus because he was happy and relieved that I'd pulled it off."

Kaia remembered how the silver-haired man had seemed…giddy was about the only way to describe it. Word got out that he'd wanted someone who could put various objects back inside his friends' homes without them finding out. He'd made up some story about why— Kaia had forgotten because it didn't matter. Royce heard about it, mentioned her name, and ultimately, that job,

and the money she'd earned, had bought her sophomore
year of college.

She remembered seeing the diamond winking at her
from an open box when Casper had unlocked his wall
safe to get her cash. She'd admired it and he'd handed
it to her. "It's yours. A cat's eye for a cat burglar."

That was what her father had just said.

A prickle of unease flashed through her, especially
when her father shook his head and said, "Oh, Kaia"
in the same tone of voice he used when she'd made a
mistake.

"What?"

"Men such as Casper Nazario do not give away anything."

"He did this time." But now she wondered if it was
his to give.

"You have the papers for it?"

"No—"

"Kaia, you can't trust a man like that."

"According to you, I can't trust anybody."

"That's right."

"I am so sick of this!" She zipped up her bulging
backpack. "I just want to be normal and have a nice,
normal life with friends and an actual job I can tell
people about."

Her father gave her a pitying look.

"Tell her, Manny," said her mother from the doorway.

"Tell me what?"

Her father rested both hands on her shoulders and
sighed. "Kaia, Kaia, Kaia."

"Papa, Papa, Papa." The words lacked rhythm because he'd insisted she call him Pa*pa* with the accent
on the second syllable.

"Get on with it, Manny," urged her mother.

"Kaia, this person you've been associating with, this Blake McCauley…"

Her heart froze. "What about him?"

"He's an officer of the law." Her father looked as though he'd just told her there was no Santa Claus.

Relief made her laugh. "I know." She shrugged away from her father's hands. "He told me."

"He *told* you? You *knew?*" her parents asked at the same time.

"Yes." She hoisted the backpack over her shoulders. "And guess what? Cops aren't so bad after all. In fact," she paused for dramatic effect as she'd seen her father do so many times before, "we love each other."

Kaia picked up the laundry bag, enjoying her parents' horrified expressions. "He'd like to meet you," she added.

"I'll just bet he would!" her father exploded.

"I'm going to warn Phillip." Kaia's mother disappeared.

"Uncle Phil is here, too?" What was this—an intervention?

"Who do you think is watching the street?" Her father pointed out the door. "Have you forgotten *everything* we've taught you?"

"Nobody needs to watch the street, Papa. All I told Blake is that you own a jewelry repair business." And maybe a little more.

"You told him the *truth?*"

"Obviously not all of it."

Her father was pacing now. The room was so tiny, he reversed direction every four steps. "Here's what we're going to do. Pack up everything you can carry. You won't be back. The situation is bad, but not unsalvageable, if we move quickly. Fortunately, we have plans in place—"

"Papa, stop. You don't have to disappear."

"I do when my daughter tells me she's in love with a policeman." He paused in front of the desk. "Do you need any of this stuff?"

She shook her head. "It's my roommate's. Here's the deal—when you're not doing anything illegal, you don't have to avoid the police. What a concept, right?"

"I don't like it." He moved to the window and pushed aside the blinds. All he was going to see was the building next door.

"What don't you like? Going legit?"

"Your situation. I don't trust him."

"You don't even know him."

Her father let the blinds fall back into place. "I don't trust you when you're with him."

Kaia knew that, but hearing him say so still hurt. "You don't trust anybody."

"And neither should you. Time to go." He reached for her laundry bag.

"No."

Something in her voice got her father's attention. Maybe it was because she hadn't shouted or struggled or pleaded. Maybe it was because she was acting like an adult who'd chosen a different life path. Maybe because he finally believed she was finished with the family business.

He straightened. They gazed at each other for a few moments, during which Kaia noticed him slip his hand into a pocket but pretended she didn't. He touched her arm, leaned in and kissed her on the forehead.

Like he ever kissed her on the forehead. She checked the pockets of her jacket. "What did you plant?"

"A number."

To a disposable cell, she knew. "I won't change my mind."

Wearing a half-smile, he gently cupped her cheek. "You can't trust him, Kaia."

"I love him."

Dropping his hand, her father headed for the door. "You can't trust love, either."

"I NEED MORE TIME." Blake McCauley sat in his car on the backside delivery area in the Brooklyn mall parking lot.

"You've had plenty of time," his captain said. "Got a meeting with the parents set?"

"No, but I'm close. Kaia's talking to them."

"And what did they say?"

"Nothing, yet. They're out of town."

"Right. She's playing you, McCauley."

Blake gazed through his windshield into the middle distance, picturing Kaia with her smoky good looks and thick black hair. And those dark eyes that drew him in and saw through him at the same time. They'd been sleeping together for weeks and for weeks there had not been one false note. Blake knew her. And ironically, since he was undercover, she knew him better than any other woman he'd ever been with.

The only thing out of tune was the story he'd been given about her. The Kaia he'd come to know and the Kaia they said she was didn't match. Not unless she was the best liar he'd ever met in his work as a police detective. And that was saying something, since working undercover had made him a pretty good liar, himself.

"She's not playing me," he said. "She didn't do it."

"She's wearing the diamond?"

Blake smiled to himself. "Yeah." Most of the time that was *all* she wore.

There was silence followed by a heavy sigh. "Start thinking with your other head, McCauley."

Blake wiped the smile off his face and sat up straighter. "I am, sir. If she stole it, why didn't she disappear when she found out I'm a cop?"

"Oh, gee, because maybe then you wouldn't suspect her? Because then she'd have a chance to warn her parents? Because then you'd argue that a member of one of the slipperiest family of jewel thieves around couldn't possibly have stolen a diamond?"

"She said it was a gift." Blake knew the words sounded weak.

"Funny. He doesn't remember it that way."

Blake shifted uncomfortably. He knew what his captain was saying was logical, but Blake's gut told him Kaia was innocent. His brain told him it wasn't his job to establish her guilt or innocence. Blake usually went with his gut.

"Look, son, you're too close to this one. We've all had that one case where our emotions got all tangled up." Blake heard a dry chuckle. "You were overdue."

"It's not that."

"She's real pretty. Of course it's that."

Blake ignored him. "I'm about to break this case. Eventually she's going to say something that will lead us to her parents." Because if anybody was guilty of stealing, they were. "Kaia never said who gave her the necklace. Maybe they did."

"We can place her at the scene."

"You can place a lot of people at the scene."

"They aren't wearing a diamond that looks like a cat's eye."

Blake closed his eyes. He was pushing it and the captain had been surprisingly lenient. Blake figured he'd used up all his superior's good will and the man's next words confirmed it.

"It's the end of the month. Time to wrap this up, McCauley."

Blake's stomach felt worse than when he'd eaten a bad burrito on a stakeout.

"Lemme do this alone," he asked. "I don't need backup."

"McCauley!" The captain spoke sharply, Blake's name a verbal slap in the face. "She's an expert at getting into and out of places that are impossible for normal human beings. You *can't* handle this by yourself."

Blake clenched his teeth. "And you just expect her to walk outside when I'm surrounded by patrol cars?"

"McCauley, I didn't suspend you when you blew your cover with her, but if you don't shut up and do your job, I'll suspend you now."

"Yes, sir." Blake didn't point out that Kaia discovering he was a cop had worked to their advantage in gaining her trust.

"We're standing by for your signal."

At that moment, Blake saw Kaia push through the beige employee exit doors by the loading docks. She was a few minutes earlier than usual, so she must not have had to close up tonight.

And it meant his backup hadn't had a chance to arrive yet. Blake glanced in the side and rearview mirrors before looking toward Kaia again. She saw him and flashed a big, excited smile. Calm and happiness seeped through him.

In that very brief moment of time, he felt that life was

perfect and all he wanted was to see her smile every day and night for the rest of his life.

He watched her walk toward him in slow motion, like a sappy commercial. He held his phone to his cheek and hesitated.

She was early. No backup was here yet. She was an escape expert.

He could warn her. He could pick her up as usual, drive right out of the parking lot and let her go. Or disappear with her. She'd know how to disappear. They could start over somewhere. Together.

"McCauley?"

"She's here," he said, because he couldn't put it off. He snapped the phone closed and got out of his car to meet her.

She was lugging a bag behind her.

"What's all this?"

"Laundry!" She laughed, dropped the bag, and launched herself at him, wrapping her arms and legs around him and kissing him with a hungry urgency.

And Blake clutched her, kissing the words, "I love you," into her mouth. Because he did. Because he could see everything clearly when he kissed her. Together, they'd go see the captain and Blake would convince the man that they'd been investigating the wrong person. He'd have to find a way to explain everything to her… but she felt so good in his arms…

He was barely aware of a thrumming, and then the sound of tires. Lights flashed outside his closed eyes.

Doors slammed and Kaia flinched, breaking their kiss.

Patrol cars surrounded them. One last door slammed and Blake looked into the eyes of his captain.

They'd already been on site, watching, during the

whole phone conversation. The captain hadn't trusted Blake. With good reason.

"Blake?" Kaia's voice sounded panicked. "What's going on?"

Blake glanced around at the men. His colleagues. His captain. They all knew what he'd been about to do. He could see the pity and contempt in their eyes.

Contempt.

And suddenly, he felt that contempt for himself. He'd not only been about to blow his career, he'd been about to *break* the law.

"Blake?" Kaia touched his arm.

Blake looked into her dark eyes and knew the moment she saw the truth.

The captain stepped forward. "I'll take it from here, McCauley."

"No. My case, my collar." Blake took Kaia's wrist and turned her around. "You have the right to remain silent—"

But she didn't. "Blake!"

And Blake knew the sound of his name filled with anguished betrayal would haunt him the rest of his life.

2

Washington, D.C.
Present day

WHEN KAIA BENNET walked into the Guardian Security
Services conference room on Friday morning and saw
Casper Nazario's lawyer sitting with her boss, she piv-
oted in an abrupt about-face and bolted for the ladies'
room. She locked the door and was standing on a toilet
seat while pushing out a ceiling panel when Tyrone La-
Salle opened the door.

"Seriously?" she asked as he pocketed the lock pick.
"Doesn't the fact that this is the women's restroom count
for anything?"

He shook his head. "Don't do it, Kaia."

"I haven't had a chance to do anything yet." She
moved the panel out of the way and looked down on
the beefy, six-foot four wall of muscle. Light reflected
off his shaved head. "I should never have taught you to
pick locks."

"You do know that Wendell installed security

grates in our duct system after you retrieved the Bailey documents last year?" he asked.

Kaia knew. Her boss had been both fascinated and horrified at the ease with which Kaia had exploited that particular vulnerability in buildings, especially supposedly secure government buildings in Washington, D.C. He'd secured the service portals to the ventilation system at Guardian, but not the air ducts themselves. He hadn't thought it necessary because the ducts weren't designed to support the weight of a typical repairman—that was why Kaia didn't allow herself to carry more than one hundred ten pounds on her five-foot four-inch, not-typical-repairman frame. She chose not to share that info with her boss.

"Of course you knew," Tyrone answered his own question. "That means you're headed somewhere else."

The rooftop, but Kaia wasn't going to tell him that.

"Or maybe you were gonna hide out in here until everybody left, except we all saw you come in…" he mused.

In a practiced move, Kaia wiped all expression from her face, something she should have done when Tyrone first opened the door.

"Rooftop?" he guessed correctly. "And then what? Have you got rappelling equipment stashed up there?"

Yes, but more important, a prepaid cell phone programmed with the number of a helicopter pilot who owed her a favor. She flexed her arm muscles and assessed the rectangular hole left by the ceiling panel.

"Don't do it, Kaia," Tyrone repeated. "Do not run. I'll beat you to the roof."

Doubtful, but he'd certainly get there before the helicopter arrived. The question was how long would it take him to break through the rooftop door after she barricaded it?

It might be fun to time him.

Her gaze skimmed the custom black suit he wore, specially tailored to accommodate overdeveloped arms and shoulder holsters. It was the same black suit all employees of Guardian Security wore, including Kaia. She hated the slick wool-blend material. Not good for climbing.

Tyler eased forward a step, his casual movement telling her he'd decided to grab her legs instead of racing up the stairs to the roof.

"Wrong choice." She shook her head. "My feet would be out of reach before you got through the stall door."

"I could shoot through the panels."

"Too noisy. And you could kill me."

"What if I don't care?"

Kaia put the ceiling panel back in place. "There is that." She hopped off the toilet and opened the stall. "Except dead cat burglars don't tell tales."

"I've noticed live ones don't, either." Tyrone leaned against the outer door to the restroom as someone tried to come in. "It's occupied," he called over his shoulder.

"The whole thing?" protested an outraged voice.

"You knew I was going to run, otherwise you wouldn't have been here so fast," Kaia said.

Tyrone cracked a smile, his dark eyes warming momentarily. "Casper Nazario's lawyer makes *me* want to run."

"He shouldn't." Kaia mock punched Tyrone's sleeve and the unyielding arm beneath it. "If I had a choice between you and ten lawyers like him, I'd still pick you."

"He's a better lawyer than I am," Tyrone said.

"He's a more experienced lawyer than you are. Slipperier. Like his boss," she added darkly.

"I'm too big to be slippery."

"And I like that about you. Tell your wife if she doesn't treat you right, you've got options."

Tyrone grunted in embarrassment and shifted his weight. Kaia made him nervous, a fact she liked to emphasize every so often just to keep him off balance.

The only time Kaia, herself, had ever been off balance, she'd had over two years in prison to regain it.

More knocking came from the door behind Tyrone. "Hurry up!"

"Use the men's," Tyrone called. "We're gonna be a while."

"It's okay. I'm over it," Kaia assured him. "Running was just a reflex. It's good to exercise my reflexes every so often. You know, to keep in practice."

"Hunh."

Tyrone reached for the door. Kaia stopped him from opening it. "I can't." She shook her head. "Whatever Casper Nazario wants, I can't do it."

"You have to. Those are the terms of your probation." Which Tyrone knew because he'd negotiated them. And he'd continued negotiating, chipping away at the length each time some government agency needed her specialized talent, off the records.

Casper Nazario was hardly with the government. "You *know* that Casper lied about giving me the Cat's Eye diamond and that's why I ended up in prison."

"It was a he-said, she-said situation."

"Only what he said wasn't true and what I said was. And he knows it." Kaia wondered if Tyrone believed her and hated that it mattered to her. It shouldn't. "I'm not going anywhere near that man or any of his minions."

"Not alone, you're not."

Every bit of self-preservation Kaia possessed was screaming "Trap!" at her. "You can't trust him."

"I know." Tyrone met her eyes with the same steady gaze she'd held for over ten silent minutes as they'd faced each other across a table in the prison's conference room during their first meeting. "But you can trust me."

It wasn't about trustworthiness. It was about dealing with an arrogant slimeball. "Why did he ask for me?" she whispered.

"Let's go find out." Tyrone raised his eyebrows at her and Kaia nodded reluctantly. "I got your back," he murmured as he opened the door.

Yeah, but what about the rest of her?

In the doorway, a young man smiled pleasantly. "Hiya, Kaia."

She hated that. Presley seemed to think he was the only one who ever thought of rhyming her name that way.

"Do you need an escort?" he asked Tyrone.

"Bite me," Kaia said, knowing he would if the situation warranted it.

Tyrone sent the kid away with a slight shake of his head and gestured for her to precede him. Kaia ignored the annoyed glares from two female coworkers as she brushed past Tyrone and walked out the door. "You know I could still get away, if I wanted."

"I don't doubt it," Tyrone said.

"Hmm, I think you do." Kaia threw a grin over her shoulder and abruptly stopped walking, causing him to stumble against her.

"Hey!" He gripped her arms both for balance and to

keep her from running away. Naturally, she'd counted on that.

Sighing heavily, Tyrone looked down. "You took my security badge." Smirking, he said, "You'll need more than that."

Kaia held up his wallet.

He blinked and his smirk turned rueful. "Not bad," he admitted as she handed it back. "What was the rest of your plan?"

Kaia nodded at the exit to the stairwell a few feet in front of them.

"Except I'd pick the lock again and I'm gettin' gooood," Tyrone bragged.

"With what? This?" Kaia held up his lock pick.

He patted his breast coat pocket in surprise, but quickly recovered. "No. This." And he removed a second pick from another pocket.

Smiling widely, Kaia relaxed for the first time since she'd seen Casper's lawyer. Tyrone was on his game today. "I'm so proud." She tossed Tyrone the pick she'd lifted in the restroom.

As he caught the pick, Tyrone said, "You taught me never to trust anyone without a backup plan."

"And you'd better have a good one if you expect me to talk to Casper's lawyer."

For all her talk, she'd known she'd end up returning to the meeting. But that didn't mean she would agree to do the job, she vowed as she walked through the door. The only bright spot, and that was because everything else about the situation was dim by comparison, was that Casper must be desperate to seek her out. What had his kleptomaniac wife stolen this time?

Kaia sat in a comfy club chair. They were using the so-called domestic room, decorated like someone's casually chic living space. Such surroundings soothed families, especially women who were hiring body-guards or couriers.

The legal weasel who sat on the chintz sofa across from her looked out of place.

She remembered him from her trial—same weasely eyes, hair coiffed like a television evangelist, and a little pointed goatee. He was dying the goatee a dark brown now, but left his temples and sideburns gray. Odd. And not in a good way.

His gaze flicked over the men in the room. "We re-quire Miss Bennet's services for a delicate matter I will detail to her in private."

"No," said Wendell and Tyrone simultaneously.

Kaia's, "No," sounded a beat later because she'd pref-aced it with, "Hell."

"As Ms. Bennet's counsel, Tyrone will stay," her boss said smoothly, and left the room, quietly closing the door behind him.

It was quite a concession on Wendell's part. Some-thing big must be up.

Tyrone settled back in a leather wing chair he liked to use. It was the power chair, being a few inches higher than the sofa cushion where the weasel sat. The dif-ference wasn't noticeable until both parties sat down. Tyrone's chair didn't give much, but anyone who sat on the sofa sank deeply and ended up with his knees higher than usual. This also resulted in an awkward power-diluting struggle to get up from the sofa at the end of the meeting. Tyrone would be standing first, in the perfect position to extend a hand to help.

It was all gamesmanship, and Kaia was for anything that diminished Alvin Rathers, aka the weasel.

He wasn't happy about Tyrone being there, but

he started talking anyway, making up a story about Casper's wife, Tina, "forgetting" to return a couple of bracelets lent to her by a jewelry designer whose chunky designs were much favored by the ladies who lunch.

Tina was a kleptomaniac, pure and simple. Kaia had figured that out right off. It was a surprise that Tina was still getting away with it all these years later.

Kaia barely listened as the weasel explained that Casper wanted the bracelets returned to the designer without anyone, especially Tina, knowing. Because, heaven forbid the man should confront his wife and get her into therapy.

Yeah, yeah. Same song, second verse.

Just like six years ago, when Casper had hired Kaia to return jewelry Tina had lifted during a summer stay in the Hamptons. In a switch for her, Kaia had broken *into* homes and left glittering baubles for their owners to find like some kind of Tiffany's Easter Bunny.

And then he'd lied and she'd gone to prison.

Did he think she'd forgotten?

"Why doesn't he just pay for the bracelets?" Kaia interrupted, earning a frown from Tyrone.

"They are not for sale," the weasel said.

Everything's for sale, Kaia thought cynically. Casper must have balked at the price. "Then—" She broke off when she felt the unsubtle pressure of Tyrone's big foot against hers.

"In any event, Mrs. Nazario has stated that she already returned the bracelets, and, indeed, they are not in the jewel safe." Alvin Rathers shifted, struggling against sinking further into the sofa. "However, Mr. Nazario has remembered that Mrs. Nazario installed a safe or safes for her personal use, ones to which Mr. Nazario does not have access."

He didn't even know how many? Kaia perked up. Okay, now *this* was great. Anything that caused Casper to suffer was great.

"It is possible that Mrs. Nazario placed the bracelets in them for safekeeping and has forgotten."

Kaia was especially proud of her restraint in letting this whopper pass unchallenged.

The weasel withdrew a legal-looking paper from his briefcase. "Mr. Nazario wishes to hire Miss Bennet to locate and open the safe and/or safes and examine the contents for these two bracelets." He placed a photograph on the coffee table and slid it toward her.

Kaia saw two wide cuffs set with a lot of turquoise chunks and some designs that looked vaguely American Indian. Strikingly beautiful, sure, but she'd been expecting diamonds at least.

"If Miss Bennet identifies said bracelets, she will—"

"Identifies to the best of her ability as a non expert," inserted Tyrone, who was studying the printed agreement.

Alvin smiled. "I'll concede the point, although a case can be made as to her expertise."

"Actually, not," Kaia said, just to keep things moving along. "I don't know anything about turquoise. That is why I'm not the person for this job. Sorry." She stood.

Tyrone spoke, "Let's acknowledge that we're all aware that prior to her employment with Guardian, Mr. Nazario retained Kaia's services—"

He made her sound like a hooker.

"—and they had a disagreement over terms."

Disagreement? She gave Tyrone a hard look. "He gave me the Cat's Eye pendant and then claimed I stole it rather than admit the truth to his wife. I went to *prison*."

"There was no record of your agree——" the weasel began.

"There will be this time," Tyrone said.

"There won't be a 'this time.' Look." Kaia held up her hand. "The thought of Casper Nazario makes me so angry my hand shakes. I can't crack a safe with shaking hands."

"Will telling you that Mr. Nazario will be paying double the fee, of which you'll receive fifty percent, help you get over the shakes?" Tyrone asked.

Kaia's hand stilled. "Yes." She sat back down. She wanted to tell herself that it wasn't just because of the money; there had to be more to this than a couple of turquoise cuffs and she was curious to discover what was really going on. But it *was* about the money.

The weasel managed to sneer without moving his lips. "Excellent decision, since I imagine the fee will be quite high due to the constraints."

"What constraints?" Kaia asked suspiciously.

"We require the utmost discretion in an extremely delicate situation." The weasel began removing folders and papers from his briefcase. "Mrs. Nazario is to remain unaware of any attempt to locate and, if located, retrieve the bracelets."

"Like she's not going to notice when they disappear?" Talk about denial.

"If so, she will not suspect Mr. Nazario, who will be in London when you search tonight."

"*Tonight* tonight? In the Hamptons?"

"No. At the Alexandria home."

Just across the river in Virginia, but still. She'd never been in that house. Trying not to be flattered that he thought so highly of her skills, Kaia shook her head at Tyrone. "I need time to study the floor plan and the security system, not to mention assemble any equipment I need. I don't even know what kind of safe—or safes—I'll be dealing with. This is a two-part job. First, I need to locate them and then come back with my equipment."

"Impossible. Tonight presents a unique opportunity and we must take advantage. You'll have access to the house." Alvin unfolded a copy of blueprints that covered the table. "Mrs. Nazario is hosting a trunk show for Royce, the designer to whom the bracelets belong."

Royce? Unreal. She hadn't had contact with Royce in years. She hadn't had contact with anyone from her former life in years.

"I've arranged for you to act as his assistant tonight."

"You want me to steal the bracelets during a party?" In spite of herself, Kaia felt her pulse quicken.

The weasel winced. "Not steal—"

Kaia waved her hand. "Words to that effect."

Some of that old feeling started pumping through her. The anticipation, the rush, the challenge and excitement. The possibility. The outrageousness of it all. Stealing jewelry from the hostess during a party. And not just any party, a *jewelry* party with extra security. If she pulled it off, it would be a high like she hadn't experienced since…since before. Since being part of her family's long, intricately planned thefts where the risk was great, but so was the payoff.

She supposed her parents and uncle were still running their cons out there. Somewhere. Without her. Because she was on the side of the law now. To be honest—ha—there wasn't a whole lot of difference on this side, except that she had to give the stuff up and her thefts were sanctioned. Tyrone saw to her legal protection and her boss assumed responsibility for her during her probation. It wasn't all out of the goodness of his heart; Kaia had made a lot of money for Guardian. And it sure beat going back to prison.

"So the designer knows what's up?" she asked, wondering if Royce had mentioned that they knew each other. Or had known each other. She wasn't admitting anything if he hadn't. That info was on a need-to-know basis and no one needed to know.

"Yes. He understands the need for discretion."

I'll bet he does. "I don't suppose we're providing security tonight."

"No," Tyrone said, neutrally. "Nor did we install the specialized features on the premises. The Nazarios are great patrons of the arts and frequently host exhibitions in conjunction with fundraisers in their home."

"You're talking museum-quality security, aren't you?" Kaia asked. "Lasers. Gates. Pressure pads. All custom. And no time to practice?" There was a difference between a challenge and an impossibility.

"I don't know the details," Tyrone said and shifted his gaze to the lawyer.

From his briefcase, Alvin had withdrawn a matte gold, silver and black folder obviously containing the system schematics. He hesitated, wearing an expression of pained conflict.

"She's bonded," Tyrone reminded him. And possibly, Kaia, too.

Just looking at the cover told Kaia that the system was first-rate. It probably cost ten bucks just to print the folder.

Carefully, the weasel set it in the middle of the coffee table. "Security was recently upgraded," he said as Kaia reached for the folder.

Joy. There was most likely some new twist she didn't

know about. "Can we consider bringing the party rent-a-cops in on this?" She lifted the edge. "I mean, come on."

"Absolutely not," Alvin said.

Kaia stared at the first page of the complex setup. What a challenge. She would have loved to have beaten this system, but without the time to properly prepare, she didn't have a chance. "If—no, when—I trip an alarm, it's going to cause a lot more attention than telling the security detail to give me access. Isn't there some sort of professional courtesy thing among security peeps?"

"As in 'look the other way while we rob your client'?" Tyrone asked. "Mmm…not that I recall."

Kaia grinned up at him. The gleam in his eyes told her he'd like nothing better than to beat the other company. She flipped through more papers. "So who got tonight's gig?"

Just as her fingers paused on a cover letter outlining the number of personnel who would be on site and the screening process for the staff and guests she heard, "Blake McCauley at TransSecure."

Kaia froze.

"TransSecure designed the system for the house, as well. That's their folder you're looking at."

Blake McCauley. Nothing in Tyrone's voice suggested the name meant anything to him other than as a competitor. She stared at the paper with the silver, black, and gold logo, and Blake McCauley's signature at the bottom, and hoped they would think she was reading the letter and not fighting to regain her balance. Yeah. She'd just been congratulating herself for never being caught off-balance except once. Blake was the once.

Blake McCauley. It had to be the same guy, because

that was just the way her day was going. Though when she'd known him, he'd been a police detective.

And her lover.

Unwanted memories flickered through her mind. His touch, mostly. Her family weren't touchers or huggers, unless they were picking someone's pocket. But from the moment she and Blake had been caught in a sudden downpour and he'd wrapped his strong arm around her shoulders, drawing her close enough to share his umbrella, she'd craved his touch. When she was in his arms, the terrible loneliness vanished. Until Blake, she hadn't realized she was lonely. She'd thought she was self-sufficient.

She'd been staring at the paper so long, her eyes started to sting. She blinked and the words slid into focus. Years ago, the need for Blake's touch had blinded her to caution and everything else. Even worse, she'd known and hadn't cared. She hadn't just been off balance; she'd completely fallen. No, Blake McCauley had been far more than just a fling. He'd been the love of her life.

Right up until he handcuffed her and sent her off to prison.

3

"I MADE IT VERY CLEAR to Mrs. Nazario that there were to be no changes to the guest list." As he spoke into the headset, Blake watched his people check-in tonight's catering staff and attach a discreet button to their uniform collar. The button was an RFID transmitter so their whereabouts could be monitored. Anyone who decided to go wandering around the house would set off an alert.

"Some lady's grandson is in town and she wants to bring him," a young voice explained.

Summer interns. Ya gotta love 'em. "Tell her no, Justin."

"But Mrs. Nazario already told her it would be okay."

Blake exhaled heavily. He'd never understand why people hired security and then did their best to sabotage it. He had very specific requirements when he agreed to a job and as a result, there had not been a single, unresolved negative incident in the five and a half years he'd been transporting and guarding valuables. A perfect record in an industry where reputation and trust were hard to earn and easy to lose, that was why he'd decided to spend this morning on site instead of letting his supervisor take care of the setup for tonight's party alone.

"I'll handle Mrs. Nazario. You vet the grandkid."

"But it's Friday!" Justin protested. "I only work a half-day on Fridays."

"How would you like to have every Friday off?"

"Wow, really?"

"Sure," Blake told him cheerfully. "And while you're at it, take Mondays through Thursdays, too."

"But…that would mean I'd work weekends."

Blake said nothing. Justin was Luke's sister's kid, a college freshman, and Luke was Blake's best supervisor. This was a favor, he reminded himself. He could stand it until…let's see; it was the end of June…when did college start up again, anyway?

As most people did, Justin filled the silence with blathering. "I mean, my weekends are… Oh. I get it. You weren't really—"

Blake inhaled.

"I'll get the info ASAP," Justin blurted out before Blake could speak.

"You do that."

Blake's hand was halfway to his earpiece when Justin yelled, "Wait—there's something else!"

"What?"

"Or…or maybe not. I don't know."

"Justin."

"Well, the designer guy is there setting up, you know? And he brought an assistant with him."

"Yes?" Blake glanced impatiently at his watch. Checking in the kitchen staff was taking too long and now Luke appeared to be having a confrontation with a delivery truck driver. Blake needed to see what that was all about.

"Except there isn't an assistant listed, you know, on the list."

Justin suddenly had all Blake's attention.

"I mean, it makes sense that he'd have one, but—"

"I'll look into it." Blake started to disconnect, then added, "Good catch." It wasn't often he found something to praise the kid for.

As he walked across the pebbled drive toward Luke and the delivery truck, Blake thumbed the keypad of a handheld computer and brought up the master list of everyone who would be present tonight.

The designer was listed as Royce—no last name. Or possibly no first name. Certainly no assistant, unless he or she was listed as a guest.

Blake touched the screen and a layout of the house appeared. He pressed the party room and an instant later, the voice of his man located there sounded in his earpiece.

"Josef."

"Do you have eyes on Royce?"

"Yes."

"Is there an assistant with him?"

"Yes, along with a mess of decorators."

"They'll be leaving. Find out if the assistant will be at the party. Anyone who stays gets tagged, including the designer."

"Copy that."

Blake stared at the room layout. There were too many exits and a whole lot of glass. He tapped the screen again.

"Josef, secure the jewelry until the room is clear."

"You got a spare man?" Josef asked.

"I'm on my way."

But just as he disconnected, the driver of the delivery van lost his cool. Luke didn't, which infuriated the man even more.

His arms waved out the window. "I've got three more setups scheduled!"

Blake ambled over, deliberately low-key. Luke was on the phone.

"What's up?"

The man erupted again as Luke met Blake's eyes and took a step away.

"I'm supposed to install an awning over the driveway! There's gonna be rain and wind tonight. There's a cool front south of here that's moving up the coast and it's causing all kinds of problems."

Involuntarily, Blake glanced skyward. "We weren't informed about an awning installation."

"I'm informing you! I'm informing you I got two other installs after this. I gotta get goin'!"

"I understand. We're verifying the job order now."

As Blake spoke, Luke caught his eye and shook his head. "Mrs. Nazario is at the spa and can't be disturbed."

Great. "Who's in charge?"

Luke cracked a smile. "You are."

"Yeah, I figured. Okay, search the van and let the man get to work." Blake scanned the area and pointed to a security camera with a view of the front entrance. "The awning will block that camera."

Luke nodded. "I'll move it."

"No," Blake said slowly with another glance at the sky. "If it does rain, then the valets will hang out under the awning making it easy for someone to slip past. Add another camera beneath the awning."

"Gotcha." Luke tapped at his phone and walked to the rear of the van where the driver waited impatiently.

Originally, Blake had only planned to be here for a few hours before heading back to his D.C. office, but he'd since decided to stay. The Nazarios had sunk a big chunk of change into a security system upgrade, which he'd designed. There had been a rash of thefts in the area and he wanted to verify that all was working correctly. Not that he thought there would be an attempt on the Nazario party tonight. In his lifetime, first as a police detective and now as a security specialist, Blake had only met one thief with the skills and audacity to hit the house tonight.

Kaia Bennet.

A memory of her face, pale with straight, dark hair, flashed in his mind as it often did when he worked a complicated job. What would she see? How would she elude the security? He caught himself trying to think the way she would think and analyze the obstacles the way she would because, even after all this time, Blake knew that he designed every system with her in mind. She was the best he'd ever encountered—as a thief *and* a lover.

Even after six years, he remembered the feel of her in his arms, her scent, her taste, and how her body fit perfectly next to his. He missed sleeping with her. Not just the sex, but actually sleeping. Something about the sound of her breathing and the weight of her body in his bed gave him the most restful nights of his life.

He thought of her smile lighting up her face when she saw him and the way it made him feel, or the way he'd felt before the night he realized it had all been a lie. She was a thief and a good one from a family of thieves.

But his time with her had felt real—more real than any relationship since. Except he hadn't had a relationship since Kaia. He'd had encounters. Empty encounters.

He was usually pretty good about remembering the thief part and forgetting the lover part. Not today. Not this week. Her last job before going to prison had been stealing a diamond pendant from the Nazarios.

His last case before quitting the force had been recovering that diamond pendant for the Nazarios.

And that's all he was going to think about that. It was done. The past.

As he headed to the large room where the party would be held, he gave a last visual sweep of the side and front entryway, noting the blind spots that would be caused by the awning. Yeah, it was a good decision to be here tonight. What with the weather, the jewelry, and all the extra people, coupled with a hostess who was playing loosey goosey with his security procedures, Luke could use the help.

Just in case.

KAIA STOOD IN THE middle of the party room and took in the huge Alexandria home. Clearly, Casper could afford to keep covering his wife's habit. Or maybe he'd simply stopped, because Kaia sure wouldn't be here if his wife had.

"Stop staring at me like that," she murmured to Royce, her gaze systematically locating all the glass-break sensors and security cameras.

"You don't look any worse after your stay in the clink."

"You sound like a movie gangster."

"I'm not up on prison slang."

Kaia glanced over her shoulder and resumed her systematic cataloging to verify that there hadn't been any changes from the schematics the weasel had given her. "Neither am I. I've been out nearly three years."

"Time off for good behavior?"

"Something like that."

She felt Royce move closer. "Are we sticking with the we've-never-met-before plan?"

"Except for those who think I'm your assistant."

"So very complicated. Why don't you become my assistant for real? You could."

"No."

Royce chuckled. There was a touch of a British accent to his voice. Fake, of course. The more expensive the jewelry, the heavier his accent.

"Oh, I think you could." He stepped away. "Kaia, look."

When she turned, he held up two rings, then closed his fingers over them. "Which one?"

It was an old game, a party trick. Her father had liked to show off his little girl's precocious ability. Kaia didn't want to play, but rather than make Royce curious about why she didn't, she answered, "The one in your left hand. It's an eleven carat pear-cut aquamarine surrounded by diamonds. The ring in your right hand is blue topaz, surrounded by white topaz, or maybe zircon, if you got a good deal."

Royce raised his eyebrows. "You haven't lost your touch."

Kaia reached for the two rings. "Neither have you." Making a costume jewelry copy of the original piece was Royce's shtick. What the clients did with it was up to them.

"So what are you doing in the security biz, Kaia? I

can understand you going legit, but not that way. Don't get me wrong, I'm grateful for your help tonight, but you have a gift. With an eye like yours, you could make a fortune as a gem buyer."

Oh, yeah. Kaia knew, but didn't feel like sharing the terms of her probation. She handed the rings back to Royce. "I need to polish my good-girl image first."

"You *have* a good-girl image?"

"See?" They both laughed and began unfolding the legs of the little round pedestals Royce would drape in black velvet and use to display his pieces.

"Sooo," Kaia began after checking that they were out of earshot of the decorators, "what's with the bracelets? Why didn't you just let Casper buy them for his wife?"

"They aren't for sale." And how interesting that he spoke without a trace of a British accent in his voice.

"Yeah, I heard that. What's the story?"

Royce pulled a table leg into position with an audible click. "We couldn't come to terms."

Kaia responded with a click of her own. "Okay, so what's the truth?"

"The cuffs are mourning jewelry." He glanced at her. "Jewelry incorporating hair of the deceased—"

"Yes, I know." And, ew.

"The value is more in the sentiment than for the stones so I wasn't sure you were aware of that particular genre," Royce explained.

"Fair enough."

"Except in this case, I reworked native American silver and turquoise, so there is quite a lot of historical value. You've seen the pictures?"

She nodded.

"The markings are a family history." He stopped working with the tables and held her gaze. "My family."

"Ohhh."

Drawing a breath, Royce concentrated on the tables. "I was entrusted with consolidating the separate pieces into the cuffs."

"So how the *hell* did Tina Nazario get your family history? And *why* the hell are you having anything to do with her!"

"Keep your voice down!" Royce shot a look around the room, but the decorators and florists were lost in their own worlds. "I can't afford to alienate Tina Nazario."

"With friends like that…"

Royce exhaled heavily. "Come on, Kaia. You know how it works."

"Oh, yeah."

"I wouldn't just lose Tina as a client, I'd lose her entire social set. And look." He gestured around. "See what she's doing for me?"

"Her way of paying for the bracelets? Which you still haven't explained how she got."

"I lent them to an exhibit of Native American jewelry with the proviso that they wouldn't be removed from the case. And then the photographers arrived and wanted to photograph Tina wearing the cuffs in the Wonder Woman pose—you know, arms crossed, ready to fend off bullets."

"Actually, I don't know, but I get the idea."

"Oh, I forgot. While some kids were watching TV after school, you had to go to cat burglar classes."

Kaia leveled a look at him. "For that you should be grateful."

"I apologize." Royce inclined his head. "I am grateful—or I will be."

"So you let them take the pictures and Tina waltzed away with the cuffs?"

"I watched. I never took my eyes off them and then a reporter wanted to ask a few questions and people wanted to see the bracelets up close. I lost sight of Tina in the crowd, and next thing I knew, she was gone."

"And when you asked for them back?"

"After my calls were finally returned, I was allowed to come here and fetch the cuffs. At that point, I was presented with two contemporary silver and turquoise bracelets. They weren't even my design." Royce looked so disgusted that Kaia had to smother a smile. "And Tina was out of the country."

"Nice." Kaia wouldn't insult him by asking if it were possible that Tina had simply been confused. It was funny—she and Tina had a lot in common what with both of them being thieves. Except for the fact that Tina was the trophy wife of the man Kaia hated most in the world, they might have been friends.

"She's borrowed before and Mr. Nazario has always paid my invoice," Royce said.

Kaia nodded. "But this time is different. I'm suddenly highly motivated to use my evil talents for the forces of good." Funny how when Tina took something, it was called *borrowing,* but when Kaia took something it was called stealing.

"I'll be in your debt." The way Royce said it, Kaia knew the sentiment carried real weight.

"Let's hope so. This is top-notch security and I'll be winging it."

It was a good story and Kaia knew Royce believed that was all there was to it. However, Casper was forking over some major bucks and had sought out Kaia, so she knew it wasn't because he cared about Royce's family history.

Casper cared about reputation and social standing, the true precious gems of his world. He was powerful enough and wealthy enough to put a reasonable spin on the loss of a couple of turquoise bracelets belonging to a moderately well-known jewelry designer.

There was something else going on here. She was not the only person in the world capable of a job like this. Casper had insisted on Kaia—the woman he'd lied about—specifically. Why would he think he could trust her after sending her to prison?

If Kaia managed to get into Tina's secret safe—which sounded like the title to a porno movie—she was going to take a look around.

She lined up the tables and shook out the velvet cloths. "These are wrinkled. Did you bring a steamer?"

"Yes. Oh, don't cluster," Royce directed, British accent back in place. "Sprinkle them lightly throughout the room."

Kaia gave him a you've-gotta-be-kidding-me look as he waved his arms around.

Whatever. Grabbing the steamer, she dutifully sidestepped one of the florists who was fussing with a centerpiece and carried the table and cloth to the far end of the room.

And while she was there, she stuck her head through the doorway. According to the floor plan, the neighboring room was a study. Now whether it was Casper's or his wife's, she didn't know, but studies were always good places for safes.

Dark wood, heavy desk. Too masculine for Tina, so it must be Casper's. Still, there were French doors on the other side of the room. Knowing where the exits were always came in handy. Holding the steamer in one hand and the plug in the other, as though looking for an electrical outlet, Kaia stepped into the study and crossed quickly to the doors. She scanned the frames and looked across the side yard to the front drive. Workers were installing an awning while a security guy attached a camera to an extension rod. Swell. Blake had everything covered. Clearly, he remembered all the little tips she'd given him thinking it would help keep him safe in his work. To her, clever ways to elude security had been pillow talk, something that excited her. To him, it had been valuable insight into a thief's mind. And incriminating evidence against her.

Oh, and let's not forget that Blake had obviously parlayed what he'd learned into an elite company designed to thwart, well, people like her.

Kaia drew a deep breath against a microscopic, but unwanted, flicker of pride.

Behind her, the door clicked softly closed.

Fixing a smile as she turned around, Kaia said, "I was looking for an outlet for the steam—er."

Casper Nazario stood in front of the door. A little grayer and no doubt a lot wealthier. She should have expected they would end up coming face-to-face because, you know, this really was turning out to be one of those this-is-your-life days.

"Hello, Kaia."

At least it wasn't *Hiya, Kaia.* "Liar, liar, pants on fire. You're not in London."

He gave a wintry smile. "I'm so glad prison didn't dull your intellect."

"It's my skills you hope weren't dulled. I suppose you're going to tell me why I'm really here?"

Casper crossed to the desk. Sitting, he unlocked the bottom drawer.

Kaia rolled her eyes. As if a four-year-old with a paper clip couldn't open a desk drawer.

"I know what you're thinking," Casper said.

Unlikely.

"But most people don't have your skills."

He was close enough. Horrors. She was becoming predictable.

He tossed a slim brochure onto the desktop. "I lock it to keep out the amateur snoopers." He opened up the laptop and plugged in a flash drive. "Go ahead." He gestured to the flyer.

It meant that Kaia would have to relocate closer to Casper and farther away from the French doors, but she might as well suck it up and see what he wanted.

A photograph of an ornately jeweled snuffbox immediately caught her attention. Fabergé, or done in that style. Setting the steamer off to one side, Kaia picked up the flyer, that turned out to be an invitation to a dinner at the Lithuanian embassy that had been held a couple of weeks ago.

"She didn't."

Casper gave her a grim look.

She gave him one right back. "Tell me Tina did not steal this."

"I don't know."

"But you suspect."

"But I suspect." At least Casper wasn't pretending any longer.

He turned the laptop around so the screen faced her.

"You know, I like how we can just cut through all the BS and be honest with each other and admit that your wife is a thief."

The muscle bulged in Casper's jaw as he clenched his teeth. Okay, enough baiting of the client. Kaia studied the article on the screen about the gift of the snuffbox from an American company to symbolize the opening of trade something or other that Kaia ignored because it wasn't important. She paged through, looking at the publicity pictures as the box was presented and then at a red-faced chef with an icing tube bent over dozens of other little boxes that looked just like it.

"We attended the dinner," Casper said. "The favors were replicas of the snuffbox made in chocolate."

"And she switched hers for the real thing?" Kaia guessed.

"Apparently. No one noticed for a couple of days."

"You are kidding." She was incredibly impressed with Tina *and* the chef.

Shaking his head, Casper withdrew a white container with a colorful seal on top from the drawer. "They're exquisite. See for yourself." He lifted the lid and the sides folded down. "I put mine in the refrigerator thinking I'd give it to our granddaughter."

Kaia caught her breath. She'd heard of edible gold leaf, but had never seen it up close. And how had the pastry chef made the "jewels" shine? Some kind of sugar? Kaia bent to study it and could see the chocolate lid glistening with moisture from condensation after being in the refrigerator. "Go ahead and put it back in the fridge before it gets ruined."

Casper folded the sides and replaced the lid. "If you don't find the real box, *I'll* be ruined."

Goody, Kaia thought.

Carefully, Casper replaced the chocolate replica in the drawer. "Officials from the Department of State are quietly interviewing all the guests who were present at the dinner that night. It's only a matter of time."

Time before someone—or several someones—said, "Hey, if you're missing something, ask Tina Nazario." Wink wink.

"So that's it." Now everything made sense. "The bracelets were an excuse for you to hire me. You really want me to find the snuffbox?"

"And the bracelets."

Kaia pushed away from the desk. "I was hired to find only the bracelets."

"I am aware of that. I will pay—"

"Not a chance." Snagging the steamer, she started walking out of the room. "If you want to expand the scope of the job, you can talk to Guardian."

"I can't do that."

"Ditto."

"Name your price," he barked.

Kaia could make a dramatic exit, or she could actually name a price. She stopped and turned, but stayed halfway across the room. She was still dressed in the black Guardian suit uniform with all the Guardian-issued equipment, including a cell phone. She pulled it out of her pocket and held it up. "You don't say another word unless my lawyer is on speaker."

Casper automatically made a sound of protest and then slumped, nodding his head.

Oh, man, was he desperate. Kaia thumbed a number. "Tyrone? We've got a situation. I'm putting you on speaker."

There was rustling in the background. "I'm recording," Tyrone said. "Who is present?"

"Me."

Kaia nodded to Casper who said heavily, "Casper Nazario."

She imagined Tyrone making faces, not that Tyrone would ever be so unprofessional. But Kaia liked to imagine it. "Mr. Nazario would like to amend the terms of his agreement with Guardian."

"Continue," Tyrone said.

Kaia waited for Casper to call in Alvin the weasel. He didn't. Holy moley. That meant she was in a most excellent bargaining position.

"While Kaia is retrieving the bracelets, I want her to catalog the contents of the safe," Casper stated.

"And/or safes," Tyrone said.

"Agreed. If she finds a certain snuffbox, I wish her to bring it to me."

"In London?" Tyrone asked, drily.

"At a time and place to be determined."

"We'll determine that now," Tyrone said. "Along with a description of the object."

Kaia really did like Tyrone.

Casper clearly did not. In fact, Kaia noticed quite a similarity between his tight, wrinkled lips and the weasel's. "At the Perking Lot, a coffee shop located within one mile of this address."

"I will not allow my client to leave the premises with any object she does not own."

Casper looked as though he was going to blow a gasket. If he did, it would make her day.

"We'll meet at the pool house at the conclusion of the party."

"I will also be present," Tyrone stated. "Kaia, you do not leave the main house without calling me first. When I arrive, I will notify you and then, and only then, will you proceed to the pool house."

Blake's people would never allow that. "If I can't get to the pool house without attracting notice, what do I do?"

Casper smiled faintly. "Leave the snuffbox in the drawer."

"Specify," Tyrone instructed.

"He's talking about his desk drawer and he keeps it locked."

"Unacceptable," Tyrone said.

"This is absurd!" Casper slapped his hands on the desk and pushed his chair back. "She'll leave it where I tell her to leave it!"

Silence.

"She will leave the object where *I* tell her to."

Atta boy, Tyrone.

Casper's gaze flicked to her. *Yeah, that's right. This time, you're not the only one with high-powered legal backing.*

"Kaia?" Tyrone prompted.

"In the vase on the third shelf, southwest corner of the room."

"In the event that Kaia is unable to take the object to the pool house at the conclusion of the party, she will leave said object in a vase on the third shelf, southwest corner of the room in which you are now present."

"Agreed," Casper snapped.

"I'll need a description of the snuffbox."

"He gave me a picture," Kaia said.

"Fax me a copy?"

Casper exhaled. "Yes, fine."

"And now, remuneration," Tyrone said.

Even though he knew she had the upper hand, Casper met her gaze with contempt.

Contempt. How. Dare. He. Anger bubbled within

her and Kaia ruthlessly contained it. "I want my name cleared. And I want the Cat's Eye. That's my price."

Casper gave a crack of laughter. He was really pushing it for a man on the verge of ruin.

"You're right. Forget it," Kaia said. "Sorry to bother you, Tyrone."

"Wait." And Casper actually chuckled. "One or the other, Kaia. Not both." And there was the contempt again.

He'd just asked her to put a price on her good name. Except, she'd never had a good name. As someone once said—perhaps Casper, himself—if she wasn't guilty of the crime for which she'd been sent to prison, she was guilty of others. True. But having her record expunged and not being subject to the restrictions of her probation would make life a lot more pleasant. And profitable.

"Clear my name," she said, sweetly. "Because, as you know, the Cat's Eye already belongs to me. You'll just be returning it."

Casper was a dangerously powerful man and Kaia was pushing him. If they didn't come to terms, she had no doubt she would meet with an "unfortunate accident" since she now knew about the snuffbox. Tyrone also knew about the snuffbox, which meant he and his family would be at risk, as well. Attorney-client privilege and Kaia being bonded wouldn't matter to Casper.

Failure wasn't an option here. Neither was refusing him, but that didn't mean Kaia was going to back down. Casper would expect it of her.

"No one knows," he said at last. "No one finds out or our agreement is null and void. Agreed?"

"Agreed," Kaia said.

4

BLAKE WALKED INTO THE main party room, stopped, and exhaled. Multiple exits. A wall of windows. Yes, he'd known all this, but the massive bouquets in six-foot urns, the cascading vines of lighting, and the dozen tables covered in black cloths were all new. The lights, okay, he got it, make those jewels sparkle—but how easy would it be to hide jewelry in the flower arrangements and retrieve it later? The jewelry had to sit on something, but the black, floor-length table cloths not only interrupted the line of sight, they provided a hiding place beneath.

Again, people hired security, and then ignored all his advice.

Blake headed toward a man with overly styled hair ending in a ponytail. Yeah, he looked like a Royce. He extended his hand. "Blake McCauley, head of security."

"Royce." The designer shook his hand with a grip that wasn't as effeminate as Blake had expected.

He gazed at the open case of jewelry that gleamed expensively, and noted the sister cases standing to one side. "I'm going to have to ask you to hold off on putting out the jewelry until the temporary staff has exited the premises." Blake accompanied this with a pleasant expression intended to convey that he wasn't asking anything, he was telling.

Royce assessed the room and consulted a fancy watch on a chain. "That won't leave me enough time to construct the displays before the guests arrive."

"There're too many people here for me to guarantee souvenirs won't walk out with them." As he spoke, both men had to step out of the way of a florist blindly carrying a huge arrangement toward the stairs. Pollen from one of flowers left a yellow trail on Blake's sleeve.

Instead of the argument that Blake expected, Royce capitulated and deftly returned the half dozen or so sparkling baubles to the case.

Blake brushed at his sleeve. "I appreciate your cooperation. Do you have an inventory sheet for me?" As he spoke, Blake scanned the room, eyes ever watchful.

Royce removed a printed list from a black folder, and handed a flash drive to him. "Here are the pieces and photographs. The drive contains the detailed specs on the stones as well as any laser IDs. Let's hope you don't need it. And I ask that you don't copy the drive or refer to it unless circumstances warrant it." And there was Blake's own pleasant this-is-not-a-request smile aimed right back at him.

Okay. Some day, if he had time, Blake might amuse himself by delving into Royce's background. A pity that it was unlikely he would ever have time. "Mind if I verify the list against the contents of the cases?"

"Yes," Royce said. "I do mind."

Tough. "You understand there can't be any claims of theft unless TransSecure certifies a piece was brought to the party."

Royce held his gaze a moment, and then shrugged and opened the first of the cases. "This will take some time."

"Perhaps your assistant can help. I was told you brought one with you." Blake made a show of looking around. "But such a person is not on my list."

"She is now," Royce said easily.

"And where is this assistant?"

"Assisting."

"If you want her to remain this evening, I'll need a name."

"Why ever does it matter?"

"Background check."

Royce chuckled. "That's hardly necessary."

He was hiding something. "How well do you know this assistant?"

"All her life. My niece, Samantha Whitefeather. Home from college, needed a summer job. She's family." Royce smiled. "You know how that goes."

Blake made a note. "Actually, I do."

Royce pointed to the open case. "Case C. Ready?"

At Blake's nod, he said, "Number forty-three, Ta-hitian pearl choker—the eighteen inch, not the fifteen inch."

Blake put a tick by the necklace Royce indicated.

"Aquamarine ring, sixteen carats."

Aquamarine was a bluish stone. There were four rings with blue stones. Blake studied the case. Sixteen carats was big, right?

Royce pointed to the ring. If Blake had packed the cases, he would have lined up the list and the jewelry in the same order.

"Aquamarine, fourteen carats with ten diamonds."

Blake ticked it off.

"Aquamarine…"

He was already impatient. Josef was supposed to be in here watching the room—where was he? For that matter, where was Royce's assistant? She could make the whole tedious process go faster.

"Pavé chocolate and yellow diamond leopard bracelet…" Blake marked it.

"The other," Royce corrected. "That's the cheetah."

For the love of—"Hang on." Blake pressed his earpiece. "Josef? Where are you?"

Across the room, Josef turned and held up his hand. Blake gestured for him to come there. "My associate will finish up," he told Royce. "I'll see what I can do to hurry the decorators along and give you some more time."

CASPER HAD ACTUALLY caved. Kaia was feeling pretty darn good as she made her way back to Royce and the hired muscle standing with him.

Sure, she totally expected Casper to try to pull something, but Tyrone had faxed him a contract addendum and wouldn't let Kaia say one word until Casper signed it and faxed it back.

Kaia almost wished Casper *would* try something. Yeah, bring it on. There was only one, tiny, hardly-any-big-deal thing standing between her and the freedom to do what she wanted—she actually had to find the snuffbox and she had to do it without anyone besides her, Tyrone, and Casper knowing about it. Shouldn't be a problem. Kaia wasn't exactly planning to announce her activities to the world.

If she got caught, things would get tricky, but not impossible, at least not for her. Casper wouldn't dare press charges because the get-out-of-jail-free pass Tyrone had made him sign was proof that he suspected his wife had stolen the box. But if Kaia got caught, she could kiss the Cat's Eye diamond pendant goodbye.

She didn't plan to get caught.

Who ever did?

"Glad you could join us," Royce said after he and the muscle initialed a list and the guy took off.

"I was looking for an outlet and then I steamed the cloths." Kaia knew Royce wasn't really griping about her being gone for so long. It was all for show and anyone who might overhear.

"And did you find everything okay?"

"Casper keeps chocolate locked in his desk drawer," Kaia said.

"Shh!" Royce darted a look around.

"Nobody's paying any attention to us. And you didn't think finding the bracelets was going to be that simple, did you?"

"Somebody might be paying attention. The place could be bugged. I get the feeling that nothing much gets past these guys." He handed her a container with velvet display stands and cubes and cylinders of various heights. "The head guy made me give him my assistant's name for a background check."

Kaia went on alert. "And did you?"

"I gave him Sam's. I hope she's been a good girl."

Kaia relaxed marginally. She'd been too smugly complacent after besting Casper. She should never get complacent. Ever. "Thanks."

"Don't mention it. Really. Don't mention it."

"Sam I am?"

Royce gave a crack of laughter that caused a little hairy dog on the landing above them to start yipping. "I don't think we need to go that far."

As Kaia watched, a woman swooped up the dog and carried it off. "That reminds me, I'm going to have to find an excuse to go upstairs and look around." Two decorators wound floral garland between the slats of the banister. One was on a ladder and the other, who'd returned from wherever she'd stashed the dog, knelt on the landing.

"I've learned that we're all going to be tagged tonight," Royce said.

"RFID?"

"I have *no* idea what you're talking about."

"Radio Frequency IDs. Little transmitters—stores use them for inventory control, passports have them embedded, the toll road tags use them," Kaia explained. "They're everywhere. You should look into getting some for your jewelry. Then when pieces walk off, you'll know where they are."

"Oh, hon, that sounds expensive and I don't have that kind of money." And how ironic that Royce was hovering over cases filled with thousands of dollars worth of jewelry.

But Kaia believed him. "And you never will if you keep giving out free samples." She gathered a stack of display stands and headed to another set of tables.

Royce made a face at her. Laughing, Kaia chose the table closest to the stairs, slipped behind a floral arrangement that cost who knew how much, and set her stands on the lower steps. Glancing around, she glided up the stairs, managing to avoid being seen by the decorators only to hear yipping and growling down at her feet.

Kaia growled back.

There was silence as dark brown eyes peered at Kaia through silky strands of blond hair that looked as though they'd been given expensive highlights. A pink tongue licked out.

"What are you doing up here?" The two decorator women regarded her suspiciously.

Kaia hardly felt it was their place to question her. "I'm supposed to tell you that Mrs. Nazario doesn't like the floral garland. She's decided to go with greenery only."

Their expressions didn't change. "Really," said the one on the ladder.

Tough crowd.

"No, not really," Kaia said sarcastically. "I'm looking for the bathroom."

"Look downstairs." They went back to fastening the garland. "I'm the only one who has permission to be upstairs," the woman who knelt added. The dog barked as if in agreement.

As Kaia glared at it, the dog stole a piece of ribbon and ran off, the spool unwinding behind it.

"Jo Jo!" The kneeling woman struggled to get up, muttering, "Stupid dog."

"I'll get her." Kaia, no fan of dogs—were any cat burglars?—headed down the hallway after Jo Jo.

Jo Jo very obligingly trotted into the master bedroom and Kaia trotted right after her.

"Hey! You shouldn't go in there!" she said and stomped her foot, scaring the dog into scurrying under the bed.

Thus, she was on hands and knees, talking baby-talk to the dog when the other woman arrived, huffing and puffing. "Jo Jo, come on out, sweetie."

The dog watched her carefully while chewing the ribbon.

"I don't know who you are, but—"

Kaia looked over her shoulder. "I'm Royce's assistant and pardon me for trying to do you a favor." She scooted backward and stood. "But hey. You're welcome to crawl under the bed after the dog." They both knew that there was no way the woman was going to fit beneath the bed.

The decorator glared at the bed with loathing. "Jo Jo's supposed to be in the hall bathroom, but she kept scratching and making such a fuss, we let her out."

Kaia smiled her best trust-me smile. "I'll get her and put her in there for you."

There was an insultingly long pause.

Her trust-me smile had never worked very well with other women.

"Just don't let her swallow any of that ribbon," the decorator said with ill grace. "She likes to eat stuff she shouldn't."

Kaia kept smiling as the sounds of Jo Jo gnawing on ribbon came from under the bed. "I'll have better luck with little Jo Jo alone."

The woman glared at her, obviously not trusting Kaia. Okay, so Miss Capri Pants was a good judge of character. They had a little stare down and it wasn't until a truly disgusting choking sound came from Jo Jo that the decorator reluctantly left the room. Kaia scooted beneath the bed. "All right, you mangy mutt, drop it!"

Startled, the dog did just that. Kaia pulled the ribbon away and then maneuvered completely under the bed with a speed that stunned Jo Jo. Kaia grabbed her and was back on her feet fast enough to allow for a quick look around the bedroom before Capri Pants became suspicious. From the plans the weasel had shown her, Kaia knew there was a wall safe behind a flat-screen TV in the bedroom, but didn't waste her time checking it out. Taking a chance, she opened the door to a closet full of suits, shut that door, and opened the next one, that was a fantasy closet that could have doubled as a guest room.

Tina's, obviously. With Jo Jo snuffling at her ear, Kaia searched the floor, finally discovering the tell-tale seam of carpet she was looking for beneath a chest. A floor safe. Had to be. But she was out of time.

She backed out, grabbed the ribbon and avoided Jo Jo's tongue. The stupid dog seemed to think Kaia was her new best friend.

Kaia was not.

She would have liked to check out the other rooms, but the decorators were already suspicious, so she carried Jo Jo down the hall. "Where's the bathroom?"

Capri Pants gave her a head nod. "On your left."

There was something else on Kaia's left—the metallic edge of a security gate recessed into the wall. A latch was on the opposite wall, a few feet before the landing overlooking the party room. Someone had tried to disguise the edge of the gate with a trellis-type stencil. Someone had not done a very good job. Probably the grumpy decorator.

This was a new wrinkle in an already-serious security system. Kaia knew that when an alarm was tripped, this gate and any other gates that had been installed, would seal off the hallway, either keeping out an intruder or trapping one until the police and security company arrived.

The gate was not on the plans the weasel had shown her. Of course not. But there was nothing to be gained by keeping the information from her, so Kaia's guess was that Alvin didn't know about it. Maybe Casper didn't, either. Kaia could see traces of Sheetrock crumbs on the edge of the carpet next to the baseboard. Either the system had been recently installed, like within the last week, or Mrs. Nazario had lazy cleaning staff.

Kaia was going to bet that the gates were new.

So where were the rest located? And how would she get around them if she tripped the alarm? Speaking of which, where were the alarms? There were certainly new ones, probably laser-powered. What fun.

Kaia took the tail-thumping Jo Jo into the bathroom, and then flushed the toilet for effect as she stood on it and ran her fingers around the window. Jo Jo gave a sharp bark of protest at being set down.

The window was a hexagon shape that looked out onto a steep dormer and a whole lot of pebbled concrete below. The window was small, so small it didn't have any sensors attached to it. Only a very slim, very athletic person would be to be able to climb out of this window.

Someone like Kaia.

Unfortunately, the bathroom was on one side of the gate and the bedroom was on the other. That meant there was something to protect in the bedroom. Kaia wasn't discounting the other rooms in that wing, either. In her experience, the master bedroom was the most common place for a safe, with a study coming second. Frankly, if Kaia were installing a safe, she'd bury it in the back yard, but that was just her. Actually, if she really had something to hide, she'd put it at the bottom of a swimming pool and disguise it as part of the maintenance filtering system.

All righty, then. Jo Jo yipped and whined. Absently, Kaia climbed off the toilet and picked up the dog, patting her before she realized what she was doing. Jo Jo licked her wrist. When she went for Kaia's ear, Kaia set her on the floor.

"Jo Jo, I should walk away from this one. Far, far away. Unfortunately, my movements are restricted. Now, girl to girl, I'll admit there was a time when that wouldn't have meant anything, but you know something? I really, really want to pull this off. You see, there was this guy. Isn't it always about a guy? Anyway, he did me wrong and I want revenge. So I'm going to stick around. See you tonight." Kaia headed for the door. "It's too bad Blake will never know that I beat his system."

"Cam 1."

"Check."

"Cam 2."

"Check."

Through his earpiece, Blake listened as Luke did the camera checks with their man in the van parked just inside the front gate at the end of the drive.

He had almost made the mistake of taking over, which would have undermined Luke's authority not only on this job, but on future jobs. Blake had already seen the looks from the crew, but he couldn't very well make a general announcement that the Nazarios were his first big client and he was here because he owed them, without implying that he didn't fully trust Luke.

The irony was that the Nazarios thought they were repaying *him*. Blake had just been doing his job—the one he used to have.

Actually…Blake leaned against the stone half-wall surrounding the kitchen herb garden and watched as the serving staff arrived and was checked in.

Actually, he'd come very close to *not* doing his job

back then. He'd been distracted by Kaia Bennet. He had nearly let her get away with a diamond pendant.

He was not proud of that. He was not proud that she'd tempted him into violating his integrity. Even now, when he thought about it—more often than he'd like to—Blake felt queasy. He'd come to his senses just in time and yet, he still second-guessed himself. Maybe it was her eyes. Or maybe it was the shock in her expression and the way the blood had left her cheeks leaving them a greenish white before going gray.

But was the shock because she hadn't fooled him?

Or because she hadn't been trying?

She was good. Really good, he reminded himself as he had countless times over the years. Trained by her family since birth. He'd made the right call. He knew he had.

It had just taken him too long.

But maybe he hadn't made the right call. And that's what had driven him away from the police force. Blake McCauley could no longer trust his instincts.

He'd started TransSecure and shortly after Kaia Bennet's trial and conviction, Alvin Rathers, the Nazarios' lawyer, had contacted him about security for a charity art exhibit. The Nazarios had passed Blake's name around their social set and that was all it took to make him the go-to guy when someone needed valuables transported.

He smiled to himself. It hadn't taken long for wealthy widows to dust off their diamonds to justify hiring a good-looking bodyguard for the evening. Sometimes Blake felt he was more of an escort service than a security company. But nobody got hurt, which was the point.

Sure he trusted Luke. Absolutely. But he felt better

being on site for the Nazarios tonight. Maybe because jewelry was involved—he didn't know. But his instincts—the ones that he still didn't quite trust—told him to be here.

"THERE JUST ISN'T any place to put your little pin." Kaia smiled up at TransSecure's hired muscle. There were two body types in the security biz—those who looked like the hired muscle they were and those who didn't. Each had their advantages. This type—no neck and overly developed shoulders—was meant to be visible and intimidating.

He'd be a lot more intimidating if he weren't blushing as he stared down at her neckline. "I, uh…"

"Anyway, I work with Royce. It'll be okay." Kaia made as if to move past him.

"Ma'am."

She sighed inwardly. It had been worth a try to avoid wearing the RFID tag. TransSecure had some poor guy stuck in a van watching a bunch of dots on a monitor as they all moved around. It also meant when Kaia's little dot went upstairs, he'd see it. And if she took it off and left it somewhere, the lack of movement would be noticed.

Inconvenient, but she'd think of something. She held out her hand. "May I at least put it some place where it doesn't show?" She smiled her best trust-me smile.

The guard smiled back. "As long as we can receive the signal."

See? Her smiles always worked better with men than with women. Watching him watch her, Kaia slowly slid her fingers beneath the bandeau neckline of her dress and punched the pin through her bra. "How's that?"

"Ma'am?" He looked dazed.

She lowered her voice. "Are you getting my signal?"

He stared at her mouth.

"Hmm?" she prompted.

"What? Oh." Blushing even more, he waved a handheld reader next to her chest and nodded. "Everything looks great. I mean—I'm getting the signal."

"Loud and strong?"

"Uh-huh."

"Good to know." Kaia smiled again, and drifted into the party room. Maybe later she'd drift back and chat with the guy about "all the security" in the house and what Royce could install to "make her feel safer" working in his showroom.

She did look good. It had been a very long time since she'd worn this dress and she never thought she'd wear it again. No ordinary evening gown, the dress could be worn any number of ways and was flowy enough to conceal the tools strapped to her legs. The metallic roping around the bodice and belt was actually real rope, should she need one, and there were pockets within pockets where small objects, like, oh, a snuffbox, could disappear. She wore leggings underneath, just in case she needed to go climbing, say through a small hexagon-shaped window in an upstairs bathroom.

Kaia normally didn't do strapless, but Royce had insisted that she be prepared to model some of his necklaces. He was acting as though he'd forgotten why she was really here. Meaning getting his bracelets back and not the other real reason—finding the snuffbox for Casper. It was complicated.

For just a moment, as she surveyed the party area, Kaia imagined her parents and uncle already working the room, being the perfect guests—as long as you ignored the stealing part.

But they weren't here. They weren't going to be here. Tonight, Kaia was on her own.

THUNDER RUMBLED IN the distance and the wind picked up.

It was dark for seven-thirty on a summer night. A Friday night. A casual meet-for-drinks-after-work date night. If you were dating. Which Blake wasn't. Dating meant planning, meant a relationship, meant commitment. Ever since Kaia, Blake had been going through a let's-not-complicate-things phase.

He sat on the decorative stones by the kitchen and watched the activity. From this vantage point, he could see through the windows where the chefs plated trays of hors d'oeurves and barked at assistants. He watched as the decorators drove off—but not before Luke had the van and personnel inspected. He sat there long enough to see that his men had changed into their dress suit uniforms, and watched the valets receive their instructions and jump to attention as the first of the guests drove up to the awning.

Time to join the party.

As he stepped from beneath the sheltered kitchen area, Blake felt the sudden coolness that heralded a storm. Twenty-four hours ago, it hadn't been on the weather radar. Now it was moving up the coast, fast and furious, but should clear out by the time the guests left.

He could hear the fabric of the dark green awning flapping and started to press his earpiece, but changed his mind. If he used the com system, all his men would hear. He punched in Luke's cell number.

"Yeah, boss?"

"The wind is kicking up. We probably ought to walk around and check wiring and connections, especially on the temporary installs."

"Already on it."

"Good." He should have known. "If you need me, I'll be observing the main room."

Blake positioned himself outside at the center of the windows showing a panoramic view of the long room. Bright lights. Lots of sparkle. A jazz quintet. Black and white clad waitstaff carrying silver trays passed through the crowd. A bartender tossed a shaker into the air and caught it to the amusement of a small group waiting for drinks. Everybody was moving, smiling, looking normal.

The addition of the large floral displays and eleven tall black columns displaying Royce's jewelry crowded the room. Yes, Blake had made a good decision to be here tonight. There was too much going on for a normal crew to keep track of.

Blake scanned the room again, marking reference points, noting the eleven display columns. Except when he counted this time, there were only ten.

He was rusty, he thought, swearing softly when he counted again and came up with eleven.

And then one of the pedestals moved and Blake saw that it wasn't a black-covered column, but a woman in a black strapless gown. A woman with beautiful, creamy shoulders. Lush dark hair twisted up in back. Strong profile. Elegant fingers deftly undoing the clasp on the necklace she wore. Red lips smiling as she held it out for another woman to admire. Gracefully side-stepping to fasten it around her neck. Raising her head to give him his first unobstructed view of her face.

He stopped breathing, not because she was a stunning beauty, although to him she was, but because after years of dreaming about her, he was staring into the face of Kaia Bennet.

5

BEFORE THE PARTY got under way, Kaia pulled out her cell phone and keyed in Tyrone's home number. She called his landline because she wasn't trying to reach Tyrone, who was on alert for her tonight; she was trying to reach his wife. Clearing her throat, she prepared to be casually friendly. And cheery. Or at least pleasant.

"Hi, Yolanda!" she gushed. Too much, too much. Way more than pleasant. Even way more than cheery. She sounded like a pathetically eager geek calling the most popular girl in school.

"Hey, girlfriend."

And that was the way to do casually friendly, even though Kaia wasn't exactly a girlfriend. But she was certainly trying.

Her court-ordered counseling sessions had led to the discovery that Kaia did not have any women friends. Technically, she didn't have *any* friends, but she was afraid of what the counselor would make her do if he found out. Practicing on Tyrone's wife was painful enough. Yolanda was nice and all that, but Kaia wasn't the meet-for-lunch-and-shop type. She was the break-into-your-house-when-you-aren't-home type.

"I wanted to thank you for letting Ty get my back tonight. I know it's your date night."

"Not a prob," Yolanda said, and Kaia could hear the TV in the background. "'Cause you know what I want."

Relaxing, Kaia grinned for real and walked toward Royce. "All I can do is steer Ty in the right direction, but it's going to be an expensive direction."

"Girl, it's our fifth wedding anniversary! For what that man makes me put up with, it had *better* be an expensive direction!"

Kaia laughed, also for real. Maybe this was how women friends talked to each other all the time. Maybe Yolanda hadn't figured out that Kaia had been ordered to find a woman friend outside of work. Maybe Ty didn't mind his wife getting chummy with an ex-con.

As Kaia reached Royce, he stepped back and she got the full effect of the animal-inspired bracelet display he'd been fussing with. She actually gasped. She, who had seen some serious jewels in her day, gasped.

"What? What?" sounded in her ear.

"Leopard," breathed Kaia. "And tiger, and zebra, oh my." The bracelets were so fine. And they looked it. They glittered with the authoritative sparkle the way only real stones could.

"Keep talking."

"I'll do better than that." Quickly, Kaia snapped a photo of the display and sent it to Yolanda. "Incoming. Check it out."

"Hey." Royce raised an eyebrow. "Did you clear photography with security?"

Kaia held the phone away with her thumb over the mouthpiece. "Hey, nothing. I'm making a sale for you."

Squealing sounded from the phone as the picture came through. "See?" she said. "That's my attorney's wife. Their anniversary is coming up and she likes your stuff."

"I hope he's a well-paid lawyer."

Kaia mentally appraised the pieces. Small diamonds, black, white, yellow and brown. Not the best quality, but they didn't have to be. The design and workmanship more than made up for it. In particular, there was a green and black snake meant to coil from elbow to shoulder that Kaia wouldn't mind owning, even if she had to pay for it. "What kind of prices are we talking?"

When Royce told her, Kaia's eyebrows raised. "That's quite the markup."

"While you were in the clink, I got popular."

"Stop it." Kaia gave him a deadly serious look. "Not funny."

Royce held up both hands, palms out.

"Kaia!" Judging by the tone of Yolanda's voice, she'd been trying to get Kaia's attention for a while.

Without looking away from Royce, Kaia spoke into the phone. "I'm here."

"I love the leopard! I *want* the leopard! I *need* the leopard!"

Royce could hear her. "It's cheetah," he murmured, looking heavenward and shaking his head.

"Which one?" Kaia asked.

Yolanda told her and Kaia pointed to the bracelet on the bottom of the artful stack.

"My mistake," Royce said. "It is leopard."

"How much?" she mouthed.

"Thirty-five," he mouthed back.

And he didn't mean hundred. "Seriously?" she mouthed again. Aloud she said to Yolanda, "Let me see what I can do. These are a little pricey." She ended the call. "What are you on?" she asked Royce. "Haven't you heard that we're in a recession?"

"I'm an artist. It's not only about the stones. It's the name and the exclusivity. I never repeat a design. Variations, sure, but each piece is unique, the workmanship impeccable, and the gold solid."

"Oh, please. Spare me the spiel. And the gold would be 22k, not solid."

"That's understood." Royce glanced up at the lights and made several minute adjustments to the bracelets and darned if they didn't sparkle that much more. "I thought the ad copy sounded great. I've found it very effective."

"Bully for you. I want a leopard bracelet and I'm not paying thirty-five."

He arched a brow. Kaia was pretty sure it was plucked. When had Royce become the sort of man who plucked his eyebrows?

"I didn't think you were paying at all," he said.

She smiled.

"For you, thirty."

"Come on, Royce. They're good people."

"How rare." He made a last pass over the display with a jeweler's cloth.

Kaia waited and then said, "You know, I don't blame you for giving my name to Casper's people—then or now."

"I never thought you did." He glanced at her. "Interesting that you should mention it while we're haggling."

Kaia made a tsking sound. "'Haggling is such a common word'." They'd both heard her father say it more than once.

"That it is." Royce stared at the stack of bracelets

and then lifted the top ones and removed the leopard bangle. After examining it, he reached for a folder and opened a monogrammed case filled with colored artist's pencils. "I might be able to make some adjustments and still maintain the integrity of a Royce original." He began sketching.

A Royce original. Kaia turned so he wouldn't see her roll her eyes. She'd known him back when he had two names and worked for her dad making copies of estate jewelry. And some of the copies were actually legit.

Kaia scanned the room, noting the unconscious straightening of the waitstaff and lights shining through the windows as cars arrived at the valet stand. Showtime.

The first guests had spilled into the room when Royce tore out a sheet of paper, held it at arm's length, squinted, and then handed it to Kaia. "Fourteen karat instead of twenty-two, with just enough sparkle to distract from the generous use of enamel. Thirty-five. Hundred."

One tenth the price. Kaia studied the sketch. "You know, Royce, this is so good, it's actually worth the price."

Royce plucked the sketch from Kaia's fingers. "What's her name?"

"Yolanda."

He wrote, "For Yolanda" and signed the sketch with a stylized "R."

Kaia took out her phone and sent a photo of the design to Yolanda. "Now, what about doing something similar with the snake for me?" she started to ask when someone called to him.

"Royce!"

He raised a hand to wave across the room. Kaia

followed his gaze and saw the beautifully groomed trophy wife of Casper Nazario, aka Tina the Klepto.

Quite an age difference between Casper and his wife. Kaia would bet that if Tina were twenty-five years older and had lost her looks, Casper wouldn't be so tolerant of her little idiosyncrasy.

"Duty calls." Royce straightened the bolo tie at his neck.

"I'll let you know what Yolanda thinks," Kaia said.

"Oh, she'll love it," he replied confidently, and spread his arms. "Tina!"

Of course, Yolanda loved it, beyond thrilled to have a Royce original designed especially for her. "He did that? Just now? After you told him about me?" she asked over and over.

"Yes." Kaia laughed. "But I've gotta go. The party's started."

Now all Kaia had to do was convince Tyrone to buy the bracelet. Because that's what a friend would do.

She ignored the unrepentant little voice inside that whined that a true friend would steal it.

Kaia put on the first of the pieces Royce wanted her to model. The heavy necklace was so not her style. A diamond pendant was her style, specifically, a small-ish yellow diamond with a black flaw that made it look like a cat's eye. And if all went her way this evening, she'd have it back.

Kaia stood silently behind the main jewelry display, observing the people, getting a feel for the rhythm of the gathering.

Since this was a trunk show, the guests would be trying on the pieces that interested them. Beneath each table was a notebook for orders and sales. Royce had given her a quick overview of his system, but she was more into acquisitions, than sales.

Her eyes were drawn to the knot of people surrounding the hostess. Tina wore a half a dozen bracelets on each arm, a ring on every finger and multiple necklaces, including one she wore as a headband. What piece would she steal as her commission tonight? If she only took one.

Bad Kaia. Tina Nazario didn't steal. She borrowed.

But whatever her faults, Tina sure knew how to throw a party. People poured in, the music was catchy, and the bartender had created colorful "jewel" drinks— diamond, sapphire, emerald, and ruby, all served with a festive rock sugar swizzle stick. If she weren't working, Kaia would have liked to taste them. Unfortunately, drinking on the job slowed her reflexes and she'd need them sharp tonight.

Was she allowed to eat the party food? Kaia wondered as a waiter carrying a silver serving platter passed by. On it quivered gelatin jewels in keeping with the theme. Maybe too much theme.

Time to circulate. Just for grins, Kaia added the snake bracelet to her upper arm, earning her a frown from Royce. She put it back. One piece at a time, he'd said. Fine.

Just as she'd attached the bracelet around the display cylinder, a woman approached.

"What a gorgeous necklace!"

Her cue. "It's one hundred thirty-two carats of matched aquamarine." She hoped Royce hadn't fudged the carat weight in the catalog. "Would you like to try it on?"

As she spoke, lights flickered and flashed, drawing

her attention to the windows. There was lightning in addition to the car headlights.

"Oh, it's that storm! The flooding and wind damage down south has been all over the news," the woman said. "They say it should move through pretty fast."

Kaia hoped so. Weather always stirred up a crowd and tonight, she didn't want anybody stirred up.

She took off the heavy necklace and sidestepped around the shorter woman, bending to fasten it around her neck.

She opened her mouth to assure the woman that it looked beautiful on her but was surprised into a genuine compliment. "Oh, the blue exactly matches your eyes! And it's such a pretty color. Royce has been using aquamarine a lot this season."

She had meant to imply that it was fashionable, but the woman looked disappointed. "Well, I wouldn't want to have what everyone else is having." She frowned and touched the necklace as though getting ready to remove it.

"No, I meant that he acquired several parcels of superior quality stones that have inspired him."

The woman looked doubtful, so Kaia caught Royce's eye and beckoned him over. He practically shot across the room, so Kaia knew either the woman or the necklace was worth serious bucks. Probably both.

"Royce, you just have to see how these stones match her eyes," Kaia said, and stepped back to let Royce do his thing.

He picked up his cue. "You're the only one I've ever seen with true aquamarine eyes. Such a unique look."

Thunder rumbled as lightning flickered and a gust of wind rattled the glass panes. Kaia gazed out to the front drive where red-coated valets jogged back from parking on the street that ran in front of the house. There was a line of cars now. Just how many people had Tina invited?

A crowd would work to Kaia's advantage. There was no way Tina could expect all the guests to use the powder room downstairs. An excellent excuse to go upstairs later, Kaia thought just as several lightning strikes lit up the outdoors.

She saw a figure standing outside looking in at the party as wind swirled the bushes and the valets scurried behind him. Probably one of the security guards. The next crack of lightning was followed by a boom of thunder that caused a few gasps, including Kaia's.

The figure was brightly illuminated for only a second this time, but it was enough to see his face clearly. Blake McCauley.

That was Blake standing out there watching the party. Watching her.

Kaia waited to feel shock or anger or bitterness—something. She'd had more of a reaction just seeing his name this morning. But maybe all the emotional hits she'd taken today had numbed her. Numb was good. She didn't need to battle any emotions this evening.

Ignoring Royce and the woman, Kaia walked over to the windows and tried to see past the reflection of the bright room into the darkness outside. If Blake was out there, he'd already seen her, so there was no point in pretending otherwise. When lightning next flashed into the shadows, the figure was gone, like a ghost—a ghost from her past, if she felt like being dramatic.

Kaia wanted to convince herself that it had been her imagination, that she'd been thinking of Blake, so she'd imagined that she'd seen him, but she was too practical. His company was on duty tonight, so it wouldn't be unreasonable for him to be here, too. And also, hadn't it just been that kind of a day? It was like old home week for her life.

So, Blake was here. And, clearly, he'd seen her and recognized her.

How should she play this? Kaia drew a deep breath, centering herself, remembering the job, which had to come first, and walked back to Royce, who was scribbling in the invoice book. The woman had gone.

"See? You're better at sales than you think," he said and snapped the book closed. "Wear the cabochon rubies next," he ordered. "And refresh your lipstick."

Had he forgotten she didn't actually work for him?

"Go, go, go." He made little shooing motions with his fingers.

Fine. Whatever. Kaia found the necklace Royce wanted her to wear and put it on. Looking at her reflection in one of a cluster of silver picture frames, she refreshed her lipstick.

Behind her, she saw a dark, distorted figure reflected in each of the shiny frames grouped on the bureau.

Blake, she thought as the figure loomed larger. Had to be. Dark and distorted described him perfectly.

ACROSS THE ROOM, Blake swallowed, his mouth dry.

Kaia.

He never thought he'd see her again, at least in person. To be honest, he'd never wanted to see her again, not with her last anguished cry of his name ringing in his ears. And now here she was in the Nazarios' house? She was clearly out for revenge. Too bad for her he'd decided to stay on site for this job.

She wouldn't be expecting him to be here, either. Blake could handle her quietly without disturbing the party guests. He wasn't a police detective any longer, and as long as she hadn't taken anything, he could let her go. *Would* let her go.

But the closer he walked toward her, the closer he wanted to be. Memories bombarded him. Blake had forgotten the strength of his attraction to Kaia. No, not forgotten. He thought he was past it. But, if possible, over time it had become more intense and more baffling. What was this hold she had over him? He did stupid, stupid things when he was around her. And he didn't care. She was like an addiction he had to fight.

Kaia Bennet wasn't a typically pretty woman. Pretty was too soft a word to describe how she looked. She was seductively attractive, alluring more than overtly sexy. Usually, time burnished memories, but in Kaia's case, his memories hadn't done her justice.

Potent. That was the word to describe Kaia Bennet. And dangerous. When he was around her, she filled his thoughts. Truthfully, he thought about her even when she wasn't around.

He couldn't believe she was here tonight. In the open. Not disguising herself as waitstaff or a parking valet. No, she was here, handling the jewels in front of everyone. Didn't they know who she was? This was the fox in the henhouse cliché come to life.

From outside, he'd studied Kaia long enough to realize that she was acting as Royce's assistant. That was bold, even for her. That meant that either the designer had lied to Blake, or Kaia had lied to the designer. Maybe both. She was the guy's niece? No way. These two were partners, probably running some scam. Too bad for Kaia that Blake had decided to be here this evening.

He drew a deep breath. His instincts, his gut, had

told him to be here tonight. It was back—the itch in his mind, the sense that something was off. It had taken six long years for him to trust that feeling again.

He pressed his earpiece. "Luke, you copy?"

"Yeah, go." Static sounded in the background as wind blew into Luke's microphone. That meant he was still outside.

"I need everything you can get on Kaia Bennet and Royce…whatever his other name is. The designer. See if they have a connection."

"K-I—"

"K-A-I-A. Bennet, one T," he spelled impatiently. Didn't the whole world know about Kaia Bennet and the Bennet family? Didn't Luke know about Blake's connection to her? Had he forgotten?

Blake's name had been in all the news stories when he'd testified. He just assumed everyone remembered. Maybe he flattered himself.

"There isn't a Kaia Bennet on the guest list," Luke said.

"There wouldn't be!" Blake snapped. "She's only one of the most legendary cat burglars of the past decade— at least she was before she went to prison. Where she should still be. Why was she paroled so early? Tell Justin to get me that info."

"Yes, sir!" Luke's exaggerated tone let Blake know he was overdoing it. Tough. He would neither acknowledge ruffling Luke's feelings nor apologize. This woman had slipped through his most stringent security procedures and he was damn well going to find out how. And why.

Across the room, Kaia fastened another necklace around her neck. Bloodred stones glistened against white skin.

Desire for her tugged at him. She was so compellingly

beautiful. How could any man in the room look at any other woman? The other women needed jewels to enhance their beauty, but Kaia didn't. Which was ironic, when he thought about it.

He surveyed her for countless minutes, making all kinds of excuses for doing so, fighting an attraction that was just as acute as the first time he'd seen her. If he were the sort of man who believed in spells, he'd claim she'd cast one on him.

If he were the sort of man who believed in love, he'd admit he'd been in love with her. Her appeal wasn't solely in the way she looked. It would have been easier for Blake if it had been. He'd expected an experienced, world-weary criminal, but she'd been skittish and almost shy. Certainly more inexperienced than he'd expected, but she made up for it with endearing enthusiasm.

In short, she hadn't been at all what he'd expected and before he'd known it, he was thinking crazy thoughts about the two of them. Crazy thoughts about being in love.

Blake shifted uncomfortably. It had been a long time since his and Kaia's story had ended, but his lust hadn't cooled. Maybe their unhappy ending had something to do with it.

He stopped fighting his fascination with her and let the emotions wash over him. *Acknowledge. Feel completely. Set aside.*

But hadn't he already felt them completely? Hadn't he set them aside?

Abruptly, Blake headed for the bar. Waving off the bartender, he helped himself to a glass of club soda and squeezed two lime and one lemon wedge into it. He gulped the first mouthful, hoping the bubbly tartness would clear his head.

She had to have cast a spell or the modern variation—drugs. Or maybe her family put something in the air, piped in some narcotic that made them irresistible into the ventilation system of their targets. Blake swallowed another mouthful and let the fizz linger on his tongue.

Kaia turned her back to him and primped in the reflection of a silver frame, drawing her red lips together and reminding him of the way they'd felt and looked as she'd drawn him—

He tossed back the rest of his drink and bit down on a lime. And then he walked over to confront Kaia Bennet.

He stopped a few feet away, uncertain as to the best approach. As he considered his options, the designer swooped between them.

"Mrs. Sanderson wants to see the rubies. Quick, take them off."

"I just put them on." Kaia turned around, an irritated look on her face quickly masked.

She'd always been good with masks.

As she raised her hands to her neck, she also raised her eyes and looked past Royce's shoulder directly at Blake.

His heart tripped a beat the moment their gazes locked. His was searching, he knew it was, and hers was as hard as black diamonds.

As she handed Royce the necklace, the designer turned to see what had captured her attention. Rather than stand there like a dummy, Blake stepped forward.

"This must be your assistant." He spoke first to gain

control of the situation and also to see if Royce would lie to him.

"Yes. Mr. McCauley, is it?"

"Blake." One name was the fashion, right?

Royce gestured. "My assistant, Samantha—" He turned toward Kaia as he spoke.

Blake didn't see her move or change expression, but somehow she tipped Royce off.

"—couldn't be here tonight, so Kaia stepped in," he finished.

"We've met," Kaia said.

They stared at each other and Blake sensed Royce looking from him to Kaia and back.

"Excellent," the designer said. "I'll be taking this to Mrs. Sanderson now." And he slipped away.

Normally, Blake would have watched him leave, but normally he wasn't face to face with Kaia's dark gaze.

Her expression revealed nothing of her thoughts and he only hoped his expression hid the chaotic feelings he battled inside.

She should be the one battling chaotic feelings. She was the one who'd broken the law and he was the one who'd upheld it. He'd been right and she'd been wrong. So why was he torn up about it and how could she continue to look icy cool?

One of them was going to have to break the silence. Blake figured he'd do it. "Does Royce know who you are?"

6

THEY'D COME face-to-face for the first time since her trial and that's what he chose to say?

"And who am I?" She was interested in Blake's answer. Who *did* he think she was? Because clearly, he'd never truly known her. Then again, she'd never truly known him.

"You're a woman who went to prison for jewel theft."

"A woman *you* sent to prison for jewel theft. It doesn't make me a thief."

"I call 'em like I see 'em."

"You need new glasses."

He stared at her for so long, she thought he might be considering her words.

"So what are you doing here, Kaia?" he asked, and she knew he hadn't considered anything.

It wasn't as though she'd been deluding herself that their relationship had meant anything to him. But for him to demonstrate so clearly that no part of it had been real—not his kisses, his touch, or any of the times he'd told her he'd loved her—hurt. A lot.

He'd been undercover. Doing a job. And she'd been

taken in completely. One look into his topaz-brown eyes and she'd been hooked. She was someone else with him, able to try on a different life. A normal life. And then came the moment when she'd told him about her family and what her childhood had been like and he hadn't run screaming into the night. Well, he wouldn't have, would he? He'd already known all about her. "I'm glad you told me," he'd said. "Because now it's your past and you're going to have a whole different future."

That was the truth. And it was also the first time they'd made love. Except, they hadn't made love; they'd had sex. That's what she needed to remember.

Kaia stared into his eyes and wondered how he'd been able to fake it for weeks without her suspecting. His eyes still looked hot and intense, that Kaia, in her inexperience, had interpreted as love, when it had been nothing more than empty desire. He'd had to play a role but that didn't mean he couldn't enjoy it.

Her parents had warned her. She'd been raised not to trust anyone. And when she'd ignored them, they'd abandoned her.

Kaia could tell a fake stone from the real thing with a glance from several feet away, but she couldn't tell empty words from true love. In fact, "You can't trust love," was the last thing her father said to her.

Even now, Blake's eyes told her nothing, but the rest of him telegraphed hostility.

And impatience. She hadn't answered his question. "What do you think I'm doing here?"

"Let's see…a private party, cases of jewels, and a member of a legendary family of cat burglars. What would you think?"

She smiled. "That it's too obvious."

Blake gestured with his chin. "Does Royce know you're a Bennet?"

"Yes."

"Does he know what the Bennets are?"

What, not *who*. "Don't most jewelers?"

"They should." Blake's nod encompassed the room. "And so should everyone here."

"I tell them my name if I'm asked. Just the way you tell them yours."

Blake made a cynical sound. "But nobody asks."

"Nope." She made the *P* pop.

"So you're hiding in plain sight."

"I'm working, not hiding." Kaia walked toward another display, this one featuring chunky, raw emeralds. The necklace was large and heavy, a statement piece that made the typical polished emeralds look prissy. Kaia liked emeralds because their flaws made them interesting and real. Too many clouded the beauty of the stone. Not enough, and the stone looked fake. Too good to be true.

Like her relationship with Blake. She'd been dazzled by the sparkle and setting, but it had been nothing more than a flawless fake.

"What kind of a scam are you and Royce running?" He'd followed her.

She clamped down on any emotional reaction to his accusation. No need to feel hurt. This time around, she knew what he thought of her. "What makes you think we're running a scam?"

"He lied."

"About what?" Kaia removed the necklace from the display and held it to her neck.

"His assistant."

"Sam? She *is* his assistant. She's just not the assistant

who's here tonight." Kaia turned her back and looked over her shoulder. Long ago, in another lifetime, he'd been turned on at the sight of her looking at him over her bare back. Tonight her back wasn't bare, but there was enough skin showing to give him a little reminder. "Fasten this for me, please?"

A beat or two went by before she felt Blake's fingers brush against her neck. Warmth buzzed through her. Kaia closed her eyes at the unexpected tingles. She'd been numb. In control. And now there were tingles.

After all Blake had done to her, she would have thought she'd be immune to his touch, especially one meant to be impersonal. As though his touch could ever be impersonal. Caressing, exciting, and betraying, yes. Impersonal, no.

"Where is she?"

Did his voice sound rough, or was that Kaia's imagination? Was it possible he was still attracted to her? This could be interesting. "Who?"

"Samantha Whitefeather, sophomore majoring in political science at Vanderbilt, GPA 3.1." Blake's breath caressed the back of her neck and the little hairs there rose in response.

Kaia squeezed her eyes shut. "On a hot date?"

"Don't you know?"

"I didn't get to see her date. He might not have been my type."

Blake was taking an incredibly long time with the necklace's lobster clasp. "Why didn't Royce give me your name when I asked?"

"I'm a last-minute sub." The way his fingers brushed her nape drove her crazy. She longed to turn and press herself to him the way she used to when they were desperate to get close to each other.

For a second there, she almost did. Wow. She hadn't seen that coming, at least not with such a punch.

She hated that she was still attracted to him. Hated that when she inhaled, she could tell he used the same soap.

"When you arrived this evening, Josef checked in a Samantha Whitefeather."

Kaia got a grip on her emotions. *Concentrate.*

Josef, the blushing kid, was in all kinds of trouble. She could hear it in Blake's voice. Once, she wouldn't have cared, especially about someone she didn't even know, but she'd grown soft working in the security biz. It was all this being around people. It made her feel things. It made her *care.* Caring made a person lose her edge.

And that's what she was going to tell the counselor the next time she saw him.

"I told your man I was Royce's assistant, and since I followed Royce in and Josef heard us discussing the displays together, *and* I'm wearing a tag, he made the reasonable assumption that I was Samantha."

"TransSecure staff doesn't make assumptions."

He hadn't asked to see her tag, which was just as well, because she might have shown him where she'd hidden it. The thought raised gooseflesh across her shoulders and chest.

Stop it! This is the man who seduced you for the sole purpose of arresting you. Tonight, you have a chance to outwit him, make a pot full of cash, and get the Cat's Eye back. Don't blow it because you've got an itch and you like the way he scratches.

Blake's fingers finally, *finally* stopped their ticklish movements and dropped away.

Kaia released the necklace she'd clutched against

her chest and felt the weight hold. She turned to look Blake in the eyes. "Did you directly ask Royce if Sam would be here, or did you *assume* that when he gave you his assistant's name, she would be the one working the party tonight?"

She saw the truth in his eyes and allowed herself to show the barest of victory smiles. "So the staff can't make assumptions, but the owner can?"

Ooo. That didn't go over well.

"Royce knew what I was asking. He deliberately misled me."

"You don't know that."

"He hid your identity. Why do you suppose he did that?"

They glared at each other as the window panes rattled and rain drummed on the fabric awning outside the front entrance.

"Maybe he wanted to avoid having me grilled when I should be doing my job." Kaia glanced around at the room. The guests seemed more interested in the weather outside than the jewels inside as they clustered in little groups facing the windows. "Maybe he wanted to avoid making a scene when his assistant is singled out by security for more than idle chit-chat at a gathering of wealthy clients and potential clients. Maybe he knows how hard it is for an ex-con to get a job."

Blake blinked, his only reaction.

"Maybe he believes in second chances," Kaia finished quietly.

"Do you?"

"No." She turned her back once more and walked away, mostly to prove that she could.

She felt off-balance again. It had been an off-balance

kind of day. Until today, she hadn't had much experience in feeling that way.

Kaia didn't want the practice.

She kept walking until she was at the far end of the room by the study door—now closed—where she'd met Casper earlier today. It was cooler and quieter at this end. Not as many people. Tina had set up a discreet conversation grouping in case someone was contemplating a serious acquisition and wanted to discuss terms with Royce. It wouldn't do for anyone in the social elite to be overheard engaged in anything as gauche as haggling even though it was done all the time. But discounts for one might not be discounts for all.

Drawing deep breaths, Kaia stood for a moment and fiddled with a display while she centered herself, focusing on the job. Then she went through her relaxation routine, visualizing the steps of the plan.

Her encounter with Blake had rattled her. She used to imagine all kinds of scenarios for their first encounter. Usually, it was some version of Blake realizing that he'd Made a Horrible Mistake.

After her arrest, she'd called the number her father had planted in her pocket that day in her dorm. "You know you can't trust anybody and you trusted a cop? What did you expect?" her parents had asked. And they'd been right. She couldn't even trust them.

What was the matter with her? It happened. She'd moved on, but her heart hadn't gotten the memo. So to harden it, Kaia spent the next several moments reliving some of the more unpleasant memories of her incarceration. Then she replayed the moment Blake had stepped out of her embrace, spun her around, and cuffed her.

Okay. Okay, enough. Now, the job. Visualize the method. The problem was the method's details were sketchy. Kaia had memorized the floor plans of the house, but as she'd discovered this afternoon, there had been changes, that she'd duly reported to Tyrone, who'd duly reported to the weasel.

It would have been nice to get an apology.

As if it would make a difference. Wasn't wanting one just more proof that she was losing her edge?

Forget the apology. What she really needed was a set of current blueprints.

Smiling vacantly, Kaia moved from group to group and described the emerald necklace while keeping an eye on Tina Nazario and simultaneously ignoring Blake. At that moment, Tina was speaking to the jazz band. Immediately, they pepped up the music, probably to distract from the weather. Next, Tina sent waiters with the jewel drinks out into the crowd.

The woman was smart. She was the sort who would install multiple safes. And she wouldn't install them all in the master bedroom.

Carrying Jo Jo, Tina moved through the room, mixing up groups, holding out an arm so women could admire the collection of bangles she wore.

It could be said that Tina was the reason Kaia had ended up in jail, but Kaia wasn't going to say it or think it. It was simply more wasted emotion. Tina was her mark tonight. Kaia needed to think like Tina to guess where she might have installed the safes.

Tina had a touch of the theatrical in her personality. The decor, her clothes, the way she piled on the jewels, a look that worked for her, her gestures, the over-the-top food and drink—this wasn't a woman who'd be content with a garden-variety floor safe in the closet. This was a woman who would install one as a decoy.

The way bracelets were coming off and on her arms,

Kaia wished Blake had tagged them instead of the guests. Keeping track of them was like trying to find the prize in a shell game. Actually, Kaia was pretty good at shell games, but Blake's security problems were not hers. She smiled to herself. She *was* one of his security problems.

She heard the scritch scratch of tiny dog nails before a joyous yipping sounded at her feet.

"Hey, Jo Jo," she said to the little ball of fur. "I see you got sprung."

Jo Jo danced around and licked her toes.

"Wow. Look at you, all gussied up." Kaia picked up the wiggling animal, holding her out of tongue's reach. Jo Jo's silky blonde hair was clipped at the top of her head with a diamond bow pin. She wore a string of diamonds on a wide black velvet ribbon as a dog collar.

"That's some serious bling, Jo Jo. Probably worth more than I make in a year. Well, maybe not this year, if your daddy comes through."

Kaia wondered if Casper was skulking about somewhere or if he had taken off to London for real. Not that it mattered.

"Jo Jo, where are you, sweetums?" Kaia heard.

Jo Jo wiggled insanely, and Kaia set her on the floor where her feet churned until she got some traction and took off.

"There she is!" Tina Nazario had a throaty, sexy voice in addition to everything else. No wonder Casper was besotted.

Tina scooped up the dog and allowed it to lick her face. Blech.

"That necklace is to die for!" squealed a woman to Kaia's left.

No kidding, she thought as everyone in the vicinity looked at her.

"These are rough-cut emeralds…" As Kaia described the necklace to the group of three women, she sensed another set of eyes on her, too. Just beyond Tina's shoulder, Blake silently watched her play jewelry salesman, his suspicious stare almost a tangible thing. She was surprised no one had remarked about the way he looked at her.

He presented a real problem unless she could find a way to either distract him or reassure him she was exactly who she claimed to be. Except she wasn't. How ironic that this time she was the one who was undercover.

Jo Jo gave a couple of squeaky yips and wiggled her way out of Tina's arms. "Jo Jo!"

The little dog made a beeline for Kaia. "Hello, Jo Jo!" Pretending delight, Kaia picked her up again.

Tina approached. "I see Jo Jo has a new friend."

Kaia scrunched her nose at Jo Jo, who tried to lick it. "We met this afternoon when I was helping Royce set up. I'm his assistant," she added, to reinforce her cover for Blake's benefit.

Tina scrutinized her way too closely for Kaia's comfort. "Jo Jo usually doesn't like strangers."

"Jo Jo has good taste," Blake said, walking toward them. He wore an admiring look that they both knew was fake, although Kaia had to admit that it was a pretty good fake.

He was a good actor. But she already knew that.

Tina clearly didn't like the competition. "Do you see the woman sitting on the end of the couch over there?" Tina gestured vaguely. "That emerald necklace is just her style." She reached for Jo Jo and Kaia gladly handed the dog over before escaping to the far side of the room.

BLAKE WATCHED HER go, torn between believing her and acknowledging that she was probably lying, an all too familiar conflict where Kaia was concerned.

She handled the jewelry like a pro—which she was, he reminded himself.

But why did he have to keep reminding himself? Why couldn't he trust his feelings?

Why did he still want to sweep her away and start over somewhere new, just the two of them?

Before Kaia, Blake had never had any trouble telling the good guys from the bad guys. Kaia had been convicted. She was a bad guy. Only—how could he have not sensed that badness in her? Sure, he knew all about psychopaths, but that didn't apply to her. She'd been so open about her life. She hadn't told him everything about her parents, but she'd shared way more than he'd expected. She had a job. She'd been going to college.

What he'd been told about her didn't fit. How could he have fallen for someone who exemplified the opposite of everything he believed in?

His captain had assured him he'd been taken in by an expert, but Blake was never one-hundred-percent sure. Not even fifty-percent sure.

He had no idea what the truth was about her now. The Bennets had disappeared off the face of the earth, obviously using different identities. Or maybe they were here tonight. Who knew?

Clearly, Tina had no idea who Kaia was and so far, his former lover was behaving herself. But she had to be thinking about going to jail for stealing from the

Nazarios. She wouldn't be human if she didn't want a little revenge.

Something he should remember concerning himself.

Blake continued to study her, hoping for a clue to the truth. As he watched, Tina's dog streaked across the room. Kaia bent and picked her up again and the dog licked her ear. Dogs had a sense about a person, didn't they?

Great. He was looking to an animated dish mop for character references.

KAIA ALLOWED AN ecstatic Jo Jo to lick her chin so she could chance a quick look at Blake. He still stared straight at her, as though they were the only people in the room.

She shivered, and excused herself from the group, leaving the emerald necklace behind.

At least he hadn't thrown her out or made a scene. That was something. Except she wasn't going to be able to do either of her jobs tonight if he kept staring at her as though he expected her to grab a bunch of jewelry and bolt from the room at any moment.

"Time for some more bling, Jo Jo." The dog went for her ear.

"Stop it."

Jo Jo settled against her. "I know you get a lot of attention," Kaia said. "So what's up with the clingy behavior? It's not like we got off to the best start."

She slowly moved toward a display, scratching Jo Jo's ears beneath the diamond bow. Sneaking a look in Blake's direction, she saw him talking to one of his men.

Finally, a distraction.

Turning her back to the room, Kaia quickly reached

into her bodice and unpinned the RFID disk from her bra. "Want some more bling, Jo Jo?" She pinned the device to the dog's velvet collar and set her down. Jo Jo scrambled off.

One problem solved.

Kaia pretended to make a minute adjustment to the display before following Jo Jo. Until she sneaked upstairs, she needed to stay close to her tag. Blake probably had her highlighted on the monitoring system.

Speaking of... She raised her eyes to his and found him back to staring at her once again. This time, she didn't look away. Earlier, his touch had awakened prickles of awareness in her. Was it all one way? Did he still feel anything for her? She knew he had once—there were some things a man just couldn't fake.

Blake stood there, a handsome hunk who saw the world in black and white, good and bad, right and wrong.

Kaia was more...colorful.

From across the room, she could tell from the set of his broad shoulders that Blake's body was tense. Without looking away from her—Kaia didn't think he even blinked—he held a hand to his ear. His lips moved.

They'd always moved really, really well, surprisingly full and tender for a man so hard everywhere else.

He tapped the earpiece he wore and lowered his hand. The entire time, he'd stared at her.

A tiny movement at his side caught her attention. Blake was moving his index finger between his thumb and middle finger, cracking the knuckle, Kaia knew. It was a habit he'd developed after breaking his finger and he did it when he was stressed.

As they stared at each other, Blake's dark gaze skimmed over her with unmistakable desire.

He shouldn't be looking at her like that and he knew it. Obviously, he thought she'd let it go unchallenged. Kaia started walking toward him. He was wrong.

7

TROUBLE IN A BLACK dress was headed his way.

Blake probably deserved it for staring at her.

As Kaia came straight toward him, he forced himself to remain motionless, feet slightly spread in the power position, even as his heart rate increased. She drew closer, her gaze fixed on his, and Blake watched the black dress mold to a body he remembered in detail. He'd been contemplating those details all night.

Kaia had the smoothest skin of any woman he'd known. She didn't get out much, after all, since most of her work occurred at night. But he'd loved to run his hands over it, liking that she'd purred like the cat burglar she was.

Purred like the cat burglar she was. Listen to him. That was just bad, as corny as anything he'd ever heard in any chick flick. Also bad was standing here waiting for her to come up to him instead of taking control of the situation.

The situation approached the edge of his personal space and kept right on going. Blake stepped back before he could stop himself. How was she able to do this to him?

Kaia's lips curved as she registered his slip. "Do I make you nervous?" she murmured, her voice throaty.

"No."

She stepped forward until they were nearly touching. One deep breath on somebody's part and they would be. He stopped breathing.

She leaned next to his ear. "Liar." Her tongue flicked his earlobe.

Blake inhaled sharply, his skin going hot and cold from just that tiny point of contact.

"You've been watching me," she whispered.

"I'd watch any thief around this much jewelry."

"Hmm." She looked up at him, so close; he couldn't focus on her face. "But I'm just a lowly jeweler's assistant."

"You've never been a lowly anything."

"Oh, yes." She moved back and deliberately looked him up and down. "I have."

He swallowed against a mouth gone suddenly dry. Her gaze moved to his throat.

He'd lost control of the encounter, not that he'd ever had it. The entire evening he'd been focused on her exclusively. Even now, he had no idea where Tina Nazario was, where Royce was, or which guests were trying on jewelry. Someone could swallow a ring. Hide a bracelet in a napkin whisked away by an unwitting catering staff. Any of these bunches of flowers could have a necklace lying in the bottom of the urn. Blake wouldn't know. He was depending on Luke one hundred percent because he'd been useless tonight, and all because of this woman.

He knew she was up to something, yet he still wanted

to draw her into his arms and crush her against his chest as he devoured her mouth.

Her mouth. Unwillingly, his gaze dropped. He'd spent hours kissing that mouth. He'd always left her skin pink from his beard no matter how soon it had been since he'd shaved.

They stood motionless. What now?

Rain blew against the windows, rattling the glass, probably setting off one of the alarms. One of his men could check into it.

"Look! The awning's going to blow over!" someone shouted.

Concerned noises rippled through the crowd, but neither he nor Kaia looked away from each other as the guests became caught up in the drama going on outside. He should be grateful for the weather because otherwise, he and Kaia standing close like this would attract all kinds of attention.

No matter what, he was not going to move away first.

And then Kaia did something really stupid. She pouted those red lips of hers in a slow, soft, tiny kiss.

Blood pounded in his head as he fought the urge to touch her. Kaia raised a finger to her lips, brushed slowly back and forth, and then hovered her finger over his mouth. He could feel the warmth, could feel the nerves in his lips respond even though she didn't touch him.

But he wanted her to. Desperately. He was mesmerized enough to forget where he was and who he was with. Lightning flashed, followed by a boom of thunder. Blake was wound so tightly, he flinched.

Kaia saw and laughed, infuriating him.

Then her head jerked. She looked down at her arm and he saw his fingers wrapped around it. Blake didn't even remember grabbing her. Instead of releasing her the way he should have, he pulled her behind one of the huge floral arrangements at the base of the stairs. The room lights dimmed and flickered, like his good sense.

He stared at her, at the taunting expression on her face. *I'm not going to let her get to me,* he thought while he moved his hands to her shoulders. And then he hauled her to his chest and kissed her, because she did get to him.

Pure electricity sizzled through him, recharging parts of him he'd thought were dead—the parts that were alive only when he was with Kaia.

No. He wrenched his mouth away almost immediately and stared at her, breathing heavily, hating her and hating himself.

"That wasn't much of a kiss," she scoffed.

She was right.

"This will be." He kissed her again, parting her lips, feeling a dangerous relief as their mouths fused together.

This was all kinds of wrong, but he needed to do it. He'd acknowledge the chemistry and get it out of the way so they could both move on. Prove to himself that his feelings were nothing more than an echo of a dead relationship. She'd been playing him then, just the way she was playing him now.

But she felt so good in his arms. So right. Why? He knew what she was; why did she fascinate him so? Why couldn't he forget her? How could he be attracted to someone who was against everything he stood for?

She tasted the same, but richer, more womanly. Desire heated his blood and burned away all sense of reason. He was right back to being that undercover investigator who'd allowed his emotions to become involved. He was listening to his heart and not his mind.

Blake stroked his hands from her shoulders to her elbows and back again. Her arms were hanging at her sides and not wrapped around him the way they should be. It slowly dawned on him that he was in this alone. She wasn't kissing him back. He pulled her lower lip into his mouth and sucked gently; something she used to love.

Nothing.

She'd manipulated him into revealing his desire while letting him know she felt nothing.

He supposed he deserved it, and yet he still wanted her. He gentled the kiss prior to pulling away and releasing her because it showed that he hadn't lost *all* control.

"Did you like that?" Her voice was a husky whisper. "Did it make you feel like a big, strong man?"

There was contempt in her voice and the set of her mouth, but Kaia's eyes were black and opaque.

"That wasn't what it was about."

"You're right. It was about showing me who's got the power. Who's stronger. Who's in charge."

She gave him a half-smile and pointed at his chest. "And you know what?" She smoothed her hand down his tie, past the end, skimmed his belt buckle and tugged down his zipper. Then she slipped her hand inside and grabbed his balls. "It's not you."

She'd shocked him.

Blake had a surreal moment. "Ka—"

She squeezed.

He couldn't stop the gasp. No man would have been able to. "Hey, now." He tried to move away, but she tightened her grip, not hard enough to cause damage, but she definitely had his attention.

Her expression never changed.

Blake was unnerved and there wasn't much that un-nerved him. This wasn't the Kaia he knew. Had he ever truly known her?

The pressure from her hand increased slowly. But relentlessly.

My God, what's she going to do?

He inhaled through clenched teeth. "Let go," he commanded with all the authority he could muster. It wasn't much.

"No." Black eyes. Blank face. Firm grip. *What are you going to do about it?* went unsaid.

And what was he going to do? What could he do? She'd positioned herself perfectly. He had no leverage and no way to reach for his gun. Push her away? No. Blake broke into a cold sweat. *Clearly,* he was facing a very angry woman who was letting him know just how angry she was in a way that left no doubt.

They stood like that for an eternity. Eventually, they'd be discovered, and he'd be embarrassed, but the loss of his pride was currently number three on his list of priorities. Numbers one and two were in Kaia's hand. "This isn't funny," he said.

"I'm not laughing."

"It's not sexy."

"It's not about sex. It's about power. Isn't that what you were just showing me?"

No. He'd been responding to an overwhelming attraction. To her. He thought it had been mutual and the mistake was costing him dearly. Now wasn't the time to explain or argue or demand. Now was the time to grovel. Blake had never been a good groveler. "I'm sorry."

She looked into his eyes. "For what?"

"Kissing you."

"Not yet you're not." And she squeezed ever so slightly.

It was enough. "Kaia!" He gritted his teeth. "Let go *now*."

Her lips tilted upward. "When I'm ready."

Blake fought to keep his breathing even. "I apologized. You've made your point."

"Oh, I know. Now it's about making sure you won't forget my point."

No way would he ever forget this moment. They were standing, partially hidden from the room, but someone was bound to wander by soon. If that happened, Blake knew with absolute certainty that Kaia wouldn't flinch—or let him go.

Sweat trickled from his armpits and down his spine as Blake imagined scenarios from having his own men rescue him to being caught by Tina, his most important client. "So is this payback?"

Smiling, Kaia raised her chin until her mouth was close to his and her breath caressed his lips. And damn it, he felt himself growing hard. "This doesn't *begin* to pay you back."

Okay, he got it. He really got it. He'd humiliated her; now she was humiliating him. Enough. "Release me, or you'll regret this."

"Go ahead. Call your people." She tugged. "Tell them I've got their boss by the balls."

He'd never live it down. He swallowed. "What do you want?"

At that moment, screams sounded as the awning blew apart and pieces crashed against the windows. Blake automatically tried to turn, but could only move his head. Kaia didn't even twitch.

"Kaia, I need to help out in there! Tell me what you want so we can end this."

Her gaze never wavered. "I've got a new life." She released him. "Stay out of it."

Blake stepped back. Thank God. He tried not to react as relief flooded through him, but his hands fumbled with the zipper as he closed his fly. "Stay on the straight and narrow and I will."

Without responding, she walked past him to the stairs.

"Where are you going?" he asked.

Her lip curled. "To wash my hands."

A little parting punch to the gut.

Even though he should be with Luke helping to keep things calm while they checked outside for damage, Blake watched her climb the stairs, his emotions in a turmoil that defied description.

Nothing like this had ever happened to him before. She'd totally blindsided him.

And he didn't hate her. God help him, he was more attracted to her than ever. How messed up was that?

Totally. It was safe to say that Kaia Bennet hated him with the white-hot heat of a thousand suns.

But at least she felt something.

As she climbed the stairs under Blake's angry gaze, Kaia was glad she wore a long dress because it hid her shaking knees.

If Blake had seen them he would have thought she was afraid, but she knew from past experience that an abundance of adrenaline let loose all at once caused the shakes. She'd kept her emotions in check and now all that pent-up energy had to go somewhere. Right now, she was headed to the upstairs bathroom where she'd revel in the euphoria of besting Blake, and do a few calisthenics to work the quivering out of her muscles.

Now *that* was the kind of reunion to have with The Man Who Done Her Wrong. The thing about a bold move was that you had to commit fully or it wouldn't work. And once you started, you had to see it all the way through, which she had. *Take that, Blake McCauley.*

Blake had struggled to keep her from seeing how shocked he was. Truthfully, she'd shocked herself. She was not impulsive by nature and when she'd been walking across the room, she hadn't planned to grab him by the balls. Then again, she hadn't planned to let him kiss her, either.

And that's what keeps life interesting.

She hated it when people said that.

Kaia couldn't risk looking to see if Blake still stood at the bottom of the stairs, but she figured he'd leave her alone for a little while.

She passed by the open landing overlooking the party room and entered the enclosed part of the hallway. At this point, she was out of Blake's view unless he'd followed her up the stairs. Highly unlikely.

Surprisingly, no one was upstairs. Kaia listened at the guest bath door and then cautiously pushed it open enough to see that it was empty.

This was a bonus. Now was her best chance to search for the bracelets. She glanced back and didn't see Blake following her up the stairs, so she flipped on the bathroom light and closed the door. Hitching up her dress, she silently ran down the hall to the master bedroom closet.

The clock was ticking. At some point, Blake would notice her absence and either come looking for her or check her tag's location on the monitor. She wished he hadn't seen her go upstairs, but she couldn't have everything.

Inside the bedroom door, Kaia fastened her skirt into the waistband and withdrew a pair of sheer latex gloves from a hidden pocket. She'd already been in the bedroom today, but it would be difficult to explain her fingerprints on a safe. "I was chasing Jo Jo" would only go so far as an excuse.

The first order of business was not to look for the safe, but to plan her exit strategy.

From the floor plans, she knew that the master bedroom bath connected to a room the Nazarios had turned into a home gym and sauna.

Using a tiny LED flashlight, Kaia moved through the bathroom and noted a twin of the high, hexagon shaped window in the guest bath. That was one exit possibility, she thought, and opened the door to the gym.

Nice. Almost as nice as the one she'd had growing up. But hers had been equipped with specialty balance and strength training machines. Until she'd left home, Kaia had spent part of every day of her life in that room.

But now was not the time for sentiment. Was there ever a good time? Sentiment was wasted emotion.

Kaia crossed to the sauna, pulled open the door and discovered a nice, large window facing out over the back of the house. Beautiful landscape lighting. If it weren't storming, the view would be spectacular. The window was a bump-out with a bench in front of it, and doubly insulated, but more important, there weren't sensors on it. Kaia pressed against the glass and from what she could see, there was nothing but a sheer drop to the ground. And she'd need to break both the inner and outer windows and most likely have to use the free weights to do it. Tough, but not undoable.

Once outside, she'd have to climb up to the roof, but it wasn't as if she'd never been on a roof before. And it was doubtful anyone would think to look in the sauna until she was long gone. Or in this case, back at the party, innocent expression firmly in place.

Okay, then. On to Tina's closet. Back in the bedroom, Kaia checked to see if the hall was empty before quietly positioning the door halfway closed and wedging a piece of crumpled plastic beneath the bottom. If anyone pushed the door open, the plastic would crackle and alert her. When they checked to see what was catching on the door, she could sneak away.

Though she would prefer not to do so, Kaia closed the closet door behind her and flipped on the light.

Tina's clothes were organized by color. There was a motorized rack that rotated out of season clothes, a wall of shoes, drawers galore, racks, a three-way mirror, a little bench, a clothes steamer, and something that looked like a glass sauna, but turned out to be a climate-controlled closet for Tina's furs. There was even a flat-screen TV. What, Tina couldn't listen to the one in the bedroom? Kaia thought just before she saw the camera. Kaia was allergic to cameras. Her heart blipped until she noticed that it was pointed in a strange direction for a security camera.

Kaia picked up the remote and taking a chance, clicked it. The TV screen blinked on and she saw herself. Pressing another button started a slide show of Tina wearing outfits with the occasion and date displayed on the bottom of the screen.

Holy cow. This was one organized woman.

Was it possible she'd kept a similar record of her

souvenirs? Kaia pressed buttons, hoping to see them or discover a different file, but saw nothing helpful and acquired a serious case of shoe envy.

She turned off the TV. Earlier, when she'd had Jo Jo, Kaia had noticed a strip of carpet in a slightly different shade of taupe. It was beneath a small chest that looked like an old-fashioned pirate's treasure chest. Yeah, that Tina sure had a sense of humor. Kaia lifted the lid on the chest and discovered packages of tissue paper, cedar blocks, bags and assorted closety type supplies. Fortunately, it was all light-weight stuff. A good sign, since Tina would be moving it frequently.

Kaia pushed it aside. Under the chest was a pull ring in the floor. Bingo. She lifted the square of carpet and flooring and there was the safe. Or one of them. This was too easy.

Fortunately, it was a garden-variety floor safe with a standard dial lock package. Floor safes were usually installed in concrete on the ground floor, so Kaia knew there had to be reinforcement under the floor to keep someone from merely cutting the whole safe out. Definitely, a custom job and she guessed not one of Blake's.

She wondered how angry he was and whether she'd gone too far. But for years, she'd mentally replayed their time together and wondered how he could fake emotions for so long. And why. Okay, he thought she was a thief—but why hurt her emotionally like that?

No. She hadn't gone too far. She hadn't gone far enough.

From beneath her leggings, Kaia withdrew a Vernier ring that fit over the dial and allowed her to see more precise measurements. The interesting thing about safes was that people spent a lot of money and attention on the safe and how it was installed and then skimped on the lock. It wasn't because of the expense, it was because the higher-rated locks were more tedious to open for the person with the combination, as well. People were lazy.

Fortunately.

Opening a safe by manipulation wasn't that hard to learn. It was a matter of becoming familiar with the imperfections in manufacturing and exploiting them to line up gates in three wheels, get the fence to drop, and retract the bolt.

Kaia spun the dial to the left and got started.

NONE OF THE VALETS had been hurt when the awning had blown apart because they'd been in the den beside the kitchen area playing poker and staying out of the rain. Blake could hardly fault them. In fact, he wouldn't mind sitting in.

The awning was a total loss and only the fabric cushioning the poles had kept the windows from shattering. The alarms were reset; Tina organized an impromptu fashion show of Royce's jewelry, and everybody calmed down.

Except Blake.

He paced. He paced into the kitchen, where the catering staff clustered around a small TV and watched weather reports of wind damage and strained power grids, and back to the main gathering where he watched women "ooh" and "ahh" over a bunch of metal and shiny rocks. And he paced some more.

Thoughts of Kaia filled his head and he couldn't concentrate on the job. What was it about her that got to him? Even now, when she clearly hated him, he couldn't let go of his feelings for her. It didn't matter to him that she wasn't the same Kaia; he wanted to know the woman she was now. Never mind the fact that he didn't trust her. He didn't trust himself.

Had she come back downstairs yet? Reluctantly, he scanned the room for her. She wasn't part of the fashion show and he didn't see her. And he hadn't seen her since she'd walked upstairs after their…encounter.

That, in a weird, twisted I-don't-ever-need-to-go-through-again way, had reassured him. She was strong, and she could take care of herself.

For someone with her background, she'd been strangely naive when they'd been together. Giving and open. He thought now of her hard, opaque eyes and unsmiling red mouth. Time and experience had hardened her. Then again, time and experience had hardened him.

He shook his head as if to shake away the memories. She'd been out of his sight too long. Blake casually strolled to where Royce spoke to a couple. "Where's Kaia?" he asked. He was interrupting and he didn't care.

Irritated, Royce said in an undertone, "I sent her off to clean jewelry."

When Blake gave him a skeptical look he added, "It gets makeup smudges and lipstick smears all over it. We must keep our sparklies sparkling!" He moved off.

Okay. Blake would buy that. So how long did it take to clean jewelry?

He watched the party for another minute, and then slipped outside the room. Tapping his earpiece, he asked his man monitoring the tags to locate Kaia.

"She's in the party room."

Blake stepped into the doorway and looked. "Where?"

"According to the ID tags, she's right there by Mrs. Nazario."

Holding her dog in her lap, Tina sat at the end of a

row of chairs that had been hurriedly pushed together for the show. The man sitting next to her was not Kaia, nor was the woman sitting next to him. Or anyone sitting anywhere.

"I am looking at Mrs. Nazario and Kaia Bennet is not in sight."

"That's where her tag is—almost right on top of Mrs. Nazario."

"The only thing—" Tina's dog licked her face and Blake froze.

"Wha—"

Blake disconnected and hurried toward Tina Nazario and her little dog, already knowing what he'd find.

"Excuse me." He pulled the dog from Tina's arms. The dog growled and snapped at him.

"What are you doing to Jo Jo?" Tina demanded.

"Looking for an ID tag." Blake ran his hands around the collar.

Just as Blake's fingers touched the disk, Jo Jo wiggled like crazy and snarled. Tina looked as though she was about to snarl at him, too. Blake set the dog down and it ran off, still wearing Kaia's tag.

"Sweetums!" Tina called after her.

He'd expected to find Kaia's tag on the dog, but he still couldn't believe she'd actually try to steal something on his watch. And he'd wanted to believe her, wanted to believe she was nothing more than a jewelry designer's assistant. Actually, he'd hoped he'd been wrong about her six years ago so he could justify his unending fascination with her.

Now that he knew she'd been lying all along, it should be easier for him to forget about her.

But first, he had to find her.

8

Kaia stared into a well of jumbled jewelry and knick-knacks. The mess was so unexpected and tragic. Unexpected because of the way the rest of Tina's closet was stringently organized and tragic because the way everything had been dumped together damaged the pieces.

Kaia could imagine Tina furtively opening the safe and tossing whatever she'd stolen into the hole in the closet floor, slamming the lid on, and forgetting about it. The safe was full, too. Tina hadn't installed a secret hiding place because she was clever; she'd installed it because she needed the room.

Kaia gingerly pulled out a strand of baroque pearls, a sterling spoon, three Montblanc pens, some crystal figurines, ugly and scratched, bracelets, perfume bottles, an Hermès scarf and a ruby-red lobster claw keyring—with the keys still on it. Somebody wasn't very happy about that.

Shaking her head, Kaia peeled away layers of Tina's plunder until she spotted the blue and silver of Royce's bracelets. They seemed to be okay with only a

The Reader Service—Here's How It Works:

If offer card is missing write to: The Reader Service, P.O. Box 1867, Buffalo NY 14240-1867 or visit www.ReaderService.com

BUSINESS REPLY MAIL
FIRST-CLASS MAIL   PERMIT NO. 717   BUFFALO, NY

POSTAGE WILL BE PAID BY ADDRESSEE

THE READER SERVICE
PO BOX 1867
BUFFALO NY 14240-9952

NO POSTAGE
NECESSARY
IF MAILED
IN THE
UNITED STATES

H-B-07/11

GET FREE BOOKS and FREE GIFTS
WHEN YOU PLAY THE...

Lucky 7

Just scratch off the silver box with a coin. Then check below to see the gifts you get!

SLOT MACHINE GAME!
YES!
I have scratched off the silver box. Please send me the 2 free Harlequin® Blaze® books and 2 free gifts for which I qualify. I understand I am under no obligation to purchase any books, as explained on the back of this card.

151/351 HDL FESA

FIRST NAME

LAST NAME

ADDRESS

APT.#

CITY

STATE/PROV.

ZIP/POSTAL CODE

7 7 7	Worth TWO FREE BOOKS plus 2 FREE Mystery Gifts!
🍒🍒🍒	Worth TWO FREE BOOKS!
♣♣♣	Worth ONE FREE BOOK!
🔔🔔🍒	TRY AGAIN!

Visit us at:
www.ReaderService.com

H-B-07/11

DETACH AND MAIL CARD TODAY!

H-B-07/11

few minor scratches that could have been the result of normal wear.

Kaia set the cuffs aside and continued sorting through Tina's stash.

This was taking too much time. The longer she stayed, the greater her chance of getting caught by Blake. At least she had Royce's bracelets. But the snuff-box wasn't in this safe.

Casper had wanted an inventory of what Tina had hidden, so Kaia quickly videoed everything with the camera on her cell phone and returned all except Royce's bracelets. She didn't worry about the order everything went back into the safe—there hadn't been any order. Did Tina ever look at the stuff after she'd stashed it? Take it out and admire it? Kaia doubted she'd realize the cuffs were gone or even remember that she'd taken them in the first place.

Kaia fastened the cuffs into one of the hidden pockets in her skirt and searched the closet for safe number two.

It had to be close by. She checked the bathroom, tapped floor tiles, searched the bedroom, and even looked in the chimney of the gas fireplace.

Nothing. Therefore, the other safe was in the closet. Had to be, cliché or not.

Kaia stood in the center of the room and pantomimed returning from an event. A fancy one with Casper in tow. His dressing area was beside this one, so Kaia imagined the two of them discussing their evening, putting on pajamas. Casper in PJs. Now there was an image she could do without, although it was preferable to imagining Casper *without* PJs.

Now Blake without PJs...Kaia drew a calming breath, willing Blake out of her mind. Focus on Tina.

Tina would have to talk, change clothes and hide the stolen goods all without alerting Casper.

If he wandered into her dressing area, the little chest could easily conceal an open safe. So what else in the closet could do the same and be conveniently accessible?

Turning in a slow circle, Kaia's gaze landed on the fur storage cabinet. It had a lock.

But not much of a lock, and seconds later, Kaia was looking at a collection of not politically correct furs as cool, dry air puffed over her skin. It was a fur refrigerator.

She couldn't resist petting a dark coat and discovered an antique silver cigarette lighter in the pocket. She checked other pockets and found most of them hiding little prizes.

Tina, Tina, Tina. Ran out of time, did you? Kaia knew she was on the right track. She tapped on the back and the sides of the cabinet, but they sounded solid. However, the bottom was raised instead of flush with the floor. Kaia knelt and pressed and pulled. The wood bottom of the closet slid toward her, revealing a safe exactly like the first one.

Maybe Tina had stumbled onto a buy one get one free sale. Either way, this safe had the same combination as the other, which was a real time-saver.

After she opened it, Kaia found it contained far fewer items, but what stood out immediately was a white container with the colorful seal of the Lithuanian embassy on top.

Kaia opened it, and the sides folded down revealing a snuffbox that looked so much like the chocolate one Casper had shown her that she actually sniffed to see if it was real.

It was.

Gorgeous, gorgeous, gorgeous. Jewel encrusted, exquisite workmanship, truly fine stones, and its provenance as a gift between countries enhanced the value.

In the palm of her hand, Kaia held an object that could cause an international incident, would surely lead to Casper's downfall, social scandal, and maybe even result in jail time for Tina. Correction, it *should* result in jail time, but Tina would never serve a day. The weasel was too good and the Nazarios were too rich.

Still. All Kaia had to do was put back one, small box and tell Casper she'd never found it. Then she'd buy some popcorn, make an anonymous tip and watch the show.

She was tempted, sooo tempted. But then she'd never get her diamond or have the fun of witnessing Casper's weasel tell whoever needed telling that Casper had made an error and Kaia was *innocent.* Well, not innocent, but at least not guilty of stealing the Cat's Eye.

Except if she put the snuffbox back, Blake would never know how much he'd wronged her.

Not that she cared what he thought any more.

After this was all over, would Casper fire TransSecure because Kaia had been able to circumvent their system without Blake knowing?

Not that she cared what happened to Blake anymore.

Or she could take Royce's bracelets *and* the pendant, assuming she found it, put the snuffbox back and watch what happened.

Kaia sat on the floor of Tina Nazario's closet and held her future in her hand. Options. She had options.

What she didn't have was time.

She stared at the snuffbox.

Okay, fine. Casper would get his box because she

wanted her name cleared. And she wanted the Cat's
Eye pendant. But really, this was about her name. Go
figure.

Kaia set the box aside while she recorded the contents of the safe in the fur cabinet. She never would
have anticipated how important clearing her name had
become. She thought she didn't care. She knew, or
thought she knew, that Tyrone believed her. Her boss
was iffy because her past guilt or innocence wasn't
important to him, only her future honesty. But Kaia
wanted to be able to look him, and Tyrone, and everyone who worked with her at Guardian right in the eye
and…

And what? Know she'd been gullible enough to be
taken in by an undercover cop? Respect her because she
was innocent? Innocence wouldn't get her any respect,
not with that bunch. Or maybe this wasn't about guilt or
innocence so much as getting caught. If Kaia had been
guilty of actually stealing the pendant, she wouldn't
have been caught. *That's* why she wanted them to know
she hadn't stolen the pendant. It was a skill thing.

Whew. For a minute there, she thought she'd gone
soft. Thought she actually *cared.* It wasn't as though
the folks at Guardian were her family or anything. She
had a family. She just hadn't seen them for six years.

Kaia finished recording the contents of the fur safe,
closed it up with the empty white box, and was going
through all the pockets when she heard whining.

Jo Jo?

Jo Jo who was wearing Kaia's RFID tag and was
now upstairs. With Kaia. This was not good. Knowing
Blake, he was probably sitting in front of some monitor watching her tag. Instead of thinking Kaia was
back downstairs, he would have watched her dot on the

screen separate from the rest of the dots and run up the stairs and into the master bedroom.

Quickly securing the snuffbox in a pocket, she crept from the closet and listened. Jo Jo saw her and yipped.

"Shh!" Of course, that only made Jo Jo whine louder, which Kaia would have known if she'd been a dog person, which she wasn't, and this was why. And yet, dogs and cats loved her.

"Go back, Jo Jo!" She snarled at the dog, hoping it would run away, but Jo Jo gave the most pitiful whimper Kaia had ever heard. Sighing, she knelt and petted the animal, feeling the little body quiver.

Kaia had a hard heart, but she wasn't inhuman. "Aw, you're scared," she whispered on a sigh and picked up the dog. "Too many people downstairs?"

Jo Jo licked the palm of her hand. "You're not getting any sympathy from me," Kaia said. "I'm not a dog person." Or an animal person. Actually, not really a people person, either.

With Jo Jo cradled on her hip, she finished frisking the coats and closed the cabinet.

Kaia was glancing around the closet to make sure she hadn't left traces of her presence when Jo Jo's body buzzed with a low growl. A second later, Kaia heard her crumpled plastic alarm crackle as someone pushed open the door.

Dropping to the ground, she shoved Jo Jo beneath some long formal gowns while urging, "Jo Jo, sweetie, please come out." Kaia hoped the dog would ignore her. Luckily, Jo Jo continued to growl. "What's got you so scared? Is it the thunder and lightning? Jo Jo doesn't like the storm?" Kaia wished whoever it was would hurry up and find her in the closet. Jo Jo wasn't exactly the world's greatest conversationalist.

The air shifted and Kaia sensed someone behind her in the closet doorway. Keeping up the pretense, she crawled forward a few inches. "Come on, Jo Jo." She reached into the dresses. "Let Kaia take you back downstairs to your mommy. You don't have to be afraid."

"Or maybe she does," said a deep male voice. Blake, as she'd expected.

"Blake!" Kaia thought her gasp sounded convincing. Not over done, but clearly audible.

He threw a glance around the closet before settling it on her. "Have you been threatening the dog now?"

She sat back on her heels. "I don't threaten anything unless it deserves to be threatened."

"Like me?" He gave her a half-smile.

"Exactly like you."

He gazed at her and as far as she could tell, he wasn't angry. Maybe curious and a little wary. Maybe ready for a truce. A truce would be good. A truce would be *great*.

"Now about this dog," he began.

Jo Jo yipped and raced out from beneath the gowns straight toward Blake. Growling, she attacked his shoe.

"Hey!" When he reached for her, she yelped and, bless her furry little heart, ran out of the closet and hid under the bed.

Way to go, Jo Jo. Kaia couldn't have planned it better.

"Oh, wonderful." She got to her feet. "Do you know how long it took me to get her out from under there this afternoon?" She marched up to Blake, glared, and continued on to the bed. "I do not have time to keep coming up here after this dog!" She got down on all fours. "Jo Jo!"

Growling sounded from beneath the bed. Excellent.

Kaia sighed for Blake's benefit and bent to look under the bed. "Jo Jo, come here, sweetie," she crooned.

"You actually expect me to believe you were in the closet to get the dog?" came Blake's voice from above her.

Kaia looked up at him. "I expect you to help me get her out from under the bed," she spoke with exaggerated sweetness. "Try moving to the other side and maybe you'll scare her toward me."

"I'm sure she'll be fine where she is." He held out a hand to help her to her feet. "And if Tina should want to find her, it'll be easy, since the dog is wearing your tag."

And here we go. "That was the idea." Kaia took his hand and got to her feet. "Jo Jo likes to run off with things and hide while she chews on them. Finding her can be a real time sink. You ought to sell Tina a tag system so she can keep track of Jo Jo." She couldn't tell if he was buying this or not. Probably not.

"It's not your job to keep track of Jo Jo," Blake pointed out.

"I know, but earlier, she nabbed an earring—she likes ears. Can you imagine if she'd run off with it? That's when I tagged her. Because, really, Blake, tagging Royce and me was overkill."

He was wearing what she called his "stern authority" mask. No matter what he was feeling or thinking, the idea was to appear confident and in control. Kaia knew him well enough to know the mask meant he was reconsidering the situation and that's what she wanted.

"Tagging a known thief is not overkill," he said.

That was a short truce. "I work for the man! You think I can't find a better opportunity to steal from him than at a party? And what do you expect *him* to do? Steal from himself?" Shaking her head, she made as if to leave the room.

Blake grabbed her arm. Okay, she really hadn't expected to get away that easily.

"He could claim something was stolen here to get the insurance money."

"And risk losing Tina as a client?" She jerked her arm out of his grasp. "Not likely."

"You could be planting something. Revenge on the Nazarios. Or you could just be plain stealing, hoping to get away with it this time." He ticked off his fingers. "You've got motivation and opportunity."

"Oh, please! Do you think I'm stupid? Oh, wait." She flung up her hands. "Of course, you do. After all, I was stupid with you."

It would have been nice if he'd jumped in with a denial, but that would have been insulting. Nice, but insulting.

She kept talking. "It would take someone a lot stupider than I am to try anything tonight with you constantly stalking me."

Blake had positioned himself so he was between her and the door. "That is how I know you weren't up here looking for the dog. She was downstairs. With me."

"So *you're* the one who scared her. Poor thing." Kaia knew she was going to have to give him a better reason for being in the bedroom or he'd never leave her alone. The truth, or a version of it was always good. "Yeah, she came up here and found me when I was getting these." As she spoke, Kaia reached through her pocket to the inner pouch with the cuffs and drew them out. "Royce sent me upstairs to get them. They're his design and he wanted to show them off. Tina modeled them for an exhibit of Native American jewelry a few weeks ago."

Blake looked skeptical.

"There are pictures. You can search for them on Google."

"Good idea." Taking out his phone, he activated the screen and tapped.

Kaia hadn't expected him to actually do it, at least not right then. He'd been upstairs with her an awfully long time. Shouldn't he be getting back to the party?

"What are the bracelets doing in your pocket?" he asked as he studied the screen.

"Fingerprints. I'll have to buff them now." She rubbed one cuff on her skirt, conscious of the weight of the snuffbox against her calf. She really, really hoped she wouldn't have to tell him about her deal with Casper. She might be forced to reveal her relationship with Guardian to get Blake to back off, but not yet. She still had a chance to bluff her way out of this.

Once upon a time, she'd told Blake about this dress and other clothing like it. Any minute now, he'd remember and—

"What else have you got in your pockets?" He'd remembered.

"A lot. I don't carry a purse." That he knew already.

He glanced up. "Show me."

She indicated his phone. "Didn't you see the picture of Tina and Royce?" She held up one of the cuffs. "Notice the match?"

"Yes." He turned off the phone's screen. "Show me, anyway."

This was not the situation Kaia wanted to be in.

What were the chances of convincing Blake that the snuffbox was a really fancy breath mint holder?

Nil. For now, all she could do was stall and hope

somebody called him on his earpiece or, wonder of wonders, he believed her.

An interruption was more likely. Carefully, she placed the cuffs on the bedspread, near enough to the edge that she might be able to knock one to the floor, if she needed the distraction, but not so close that Blake would think she'd done it on purpose.

Next, she reached into a side pocket, going for the easy stuff first. "Money clip, lipstick, keys, tissues." She pulled the pocket inside out to show it was empty.

"Keep going."

She tossed the items onto the bed and reached into another pocket. "Jeweler's loupe, latex gloves—"

"I don't know another woman who would carry latex gloves to a party."

"It's not a party for me. I'm working."

"That's what I'm afraid of."

Was that a touch of humor? Kaia didn't want humor. She wanted Blake stern and unreasonable and using that deliberately neutral voice she hated. Hate. That's what she wanted to feel, if she had to feel anything. And she didn't—shouldn't.

"The gloves keep fingerprints off the jewelry." For jewelry, they should be cotton, but she was counting on Blake not catching that. Luckily, she actually had a small polishing cloth with her, that she pulled out to show him before dropping it onto the bed with the other stuff.

He nodded to the pocket. "What else have you got in there?"

"Keys." The fob on the ring was a tool set in the shape of a key, but she wasn't going to point that out. Next, she pulled out a small pen, that was actually a mini blowtorch, one more thing she hoped he wouldn't notice. And her other pen was a flashlight. She didn't have a real pen.

"Let me see that." He held out his hand and she dropped the light into his palm.

"Nice," he said, after examining it. Leaning forward, he carefully placed it onto the bed.

Jo Jo growled.

Smothering a smile, Kaia held up her phone. "My cell."

"I'll take that." Blake reached for it.

Kaia snatched it away. "Not without a court order."

He raised his eyebrows. "Oh, I think—"

"Not without a court order." She put the phone away. "I have confidential client data on this phone." Not Royce's clients, but the principle was the same. "You're not a cop anymore, Blake. Should you confiscate my phone, it would be a gross overreach of your authority. I guarantee you would be sued and you would lose." She let that sink in. "Even if you were still a cop, any information you found on my phone would be inadmissible in court."

He blinked, finally showing emotion in his carefully blank face. "True. You've been studying."

"I had time." She'd never spoken to him like that before and could tell it surprised him. *Yeah, Blake, I'm not the same little girl who deferred to everything you said or did.* "And I'm only showing you what's in my pockets so you'll leave me alone."

She pulled out her Vernier ring and tossed it onto the bed. "Yes, I used it when I opened safes, but now it's a ring sizer." She gazed at him steadily, hoping he didn't know anything about sizing rings.

Blake stared at the items on the bed. In the silence,

Jo Jo growled louder, probably reacting to Kaia's raised voice.

"You've got an explanation for everything." He drew his hands to his hips and regarded her through slightly narrowed eyes. "I guess that's what makes you so good."

Kaia maintained eye contact. "Or I could be telling the truth."

"Maybe."

At least she'd planted doubt in his mind. *Reasonable doubt.* Wasn't that what it was called? Something her inexperienced court-appointed attorney hadn't been able to achieve.

"But I'm not convinced," he said.

"You never were."

A couple of beats went by before he slowly shook his head.

Kaia wanted to scream in frustration. It didn't help that technically, this time Blake was right.

"Is that all you're carrying?" he asked.

All she intended to show him. "There are a few bits and pieces for emergency repairs in the bottom of the pocket." She held it open for him to look, but he remained several steps away.

"And?" He just would not give up.

"And nothing."

In the background, the jazz band amped up the music. She and Blake had been away from the party a long time, but if she pointed it out, he'd get suspicious. Like he wasn't already suspicious?

Still, why hadn't he hustled her downstairs or called for one of his security guards? Or *called* Royce. Or Tina.

Did anyone know he was upstairs?

Interesting. She'd assumed his intense gaze was

because he was trying to decide whether or not to believe her, but maybe it was something else. Maybe he was intrigued that she'd stood up to him.

Maybe she hadn't obliterated his desire for her.

Warmth rushed through her. No. She did not feel desire for him. She *would* not feel desire for him. She was in control of her emotions and she'd decide when and where and with whom she'd feel desire. Now was not the time, the place, and certainly not the person.

Beneath the music she heard a tiny sound. A pop. Blake was cracking his finger. He wasn't as detached as he wanted her to believe.

Was it possible he was still attracted to her? Still? If so, it was a weakness she could use against him, maybe play the distract-with-sex card. So what if it was obvious? That didn't mean it wouldn't be effective.

She softened her posture to a less belligerent one. "Are we done here?" She gave him a tiny smile and lowered her voice. "Or are you going to frisk me?"

Blake never blinked, but his gaze grew dark. "No. I'd like to reserve the right to father children at some point in the future."

Kaia gave a throaty laugh. "I just wanted your attention."

"Oh, you got it and then some." His voice deepened. "I know you were evening the score, Kaia. So consider us square now."

A rush of anger made her fingers tremble. Not even close. She knew men put a high value on the family jewels but Blake was totally clueless. Totally. "You wouldn't say that if you'd ever been in prison."

They held each other's gazes, his searching, hers determinedly opaque.

"Fair enough," he said at last. "So you're suggesting that if I let you walk out of here now we'll be even?"

They would never be even. "You act like you'd be doing me a favor."

"Looking the other way to theft is a very big favor in my world."

"That is why you'd never offer to let me walk if you truly thought I was stealing," she said. "Admit it."

Long moments went by. "No," he said.

"'No' you won't admit it, or 'no' you wouldn't offer?"

"Are you asking me to let you go?" he countered.

Would he? With a flash of insight, Kaia knew that if Blake were the kind of man who would do such a thing, she wouldn't have once loved him.

"You don't have any reason not to let me go." She held her arms wide. "Go ahead. Check for yourself." She was taking a huge chance. What if he did start to search her?

Then…then she'd kiss him. That was her plan. All of it. Simple, but it had its good points.

His gaze traveled over her and Kaia waited, heart pounding, actually hoping that he would touch her so she'd have an excuse to end up in his arms.

Blake's expression told her he hoped the same thing.

"I'm safer standing where I am." His voice was rough. His finger cracked.

If she hadn't heard the tiny sound, Kaia might have gathered her things, made a remark about Royce waiting for the cuffs, and escaped from the room.

But she had heard it. For whatever reason, he still wanted her. And she…was about to be very stupid. Again. "Then I'll frisk myself."

Blake's gaze was transfixed on Kaia's hands as they began a slow descent down her sides.

Dangerous, dangerous decision, but one that made her feel more alive than she had in years. Her blood hummed. She felt confident and in control. And reckless, because who knew where this would lead?

Blake had always enjoyed her body, that is why he'd been so convincing in the role of attentive boyfriend. And she'd enjoyed his, and that was why she'd been blind to the rest of it. They could still enjoy each other, as long as she remembered that was all it was.

Kaia propped one leg on the bed and smiled to herself as her hands felt the subtle bumps of picks and other tiny tools still strapped beneath the leggings hidden by her dress. Bumps that Blake would also feel if he'd called her bluff. But Blake didn't look as if he was doing much thinking. His eyes followed her movements as though she was a puppet master controlling them.

Kaia raised the other leg, watching him watch her. If he wasn't affected, he would have stopped her, right? Or frisked her himself. She lowered her leg to the floor.

Slowly, sensuously, she turned and looked at Blake over her shoulder, her signature move to get him turned on. Other than breathing, he was completely still; not even cracking his finger anymore. His chest rose and fell faster than normal.

Excellent.

Watching him, Kaia ran her hands over her hips, nice and slow and thought she heard a whimper.

Actually, she did hear a whimper, but it was Jo Jo and not Blake.

He didn't seem to notice.

Turning to face him, she slowly moved her hands over her breasts, pulling the fabric tight.

Blake stared, unblinking. Kaia threw in a tiny

breathy moan, but immediately wished she hadn't. She didn't want to oversell it.

He swallowed, watching her hands skim her stomach and lower, and then down her thighs. She turned her palms upward. "You see? Nothing to hide." Except the snuffbox near her calf.

There was a hitch in the breath he drew. "Maybe you didn't have time to take anything."

"Now you're insulting me."

"Kaia." He exhaled her name as he stared at her mouth. "I can never think straight when I'm around you."

She took a step toward him. "Then don't think."

"That's when I get into trouble." He gave her a wry smile.

"So what are you thinking now?" *Kiss me. You know you want to.*

Once he kissed her, she knew she had him. She'd make him forget where they were, make him forget his responsibilities and risk discovery. She'd manipulate him the way he'd manipulated her.

She couldn't hurt him the way she'd been hurt because a person had to care to be hurt and Blake didn't care.

But she did. Still.

But she'd be okay as long as she remained in control, that meant they needed to move this along while she could still pull it off. Maybe she should kiss him, except it was important for him to make the first move. She gazed at his broad shoulders and wide jaw and the short hair she'd teased him into growing an inch longer. Why was it was important that he make the first move, again?

Somebody needed to move.

Blake eased forward. Kaia swayed.

The bass and drums from the band directly below them reverberated through the floor with the same rhythm as her heartbeat.

Blake stared at her mouth and she knew he was locked in the same battle she was: desire versus common sense. She tilted her chin up in the slightest of invitations. *No more. He has to want you more than you want him.*

His jaw worked. She saw him swallow. His eyelids lowered. "Kaia…"

Kaia beamed "kiss me" thoughts at him. *Kissmekissmekissme.*

Stepping forward, Blake skimmed his hand along her jaw.

At his touch, Kaia shivered and closed her eyes. She couldn't help it. The combination of memories and anticipation nearly overwhelmed her. When Blake didn't go ahead and kiss her, she opened her eyes to find him gazing at her as though searching for something. He used to do that, she remembered and momentarily forgot all the bad stuff that had happened between them. She smiled, because his eyes would always light up when she smiled.

This time, they not only lit up, he smiled back and lowered his head. And then, when their mouths were just a breath away, he grimaced and pulled back.

Touching the transmitter in his ear, he said, "Yeah, go ahead."

What? No! Not now when she nearly had him.

But what were you going to do with him? a little voice asked.

Kaia sighed inwardly. Pretty much anything he wanted.

She wasn't experienced enough, hardened enough to remain completely unfeeling. Seduce him sure, but she'd get hurt all over again. Even as she was running her hands over her dress, she was remembering the feel of his palms on her skin and thinking, *maybe they could start over and forget the past...*

Forget the past? She should have her head examined. Oh, wait. She was. When her therapist had told her to find friends, this wasn't what he meant.

The interruption had saved her. Not getting tangled up with Blake again was for the best, she told herself. *Finish the job you were hired to do and go on with your life. Leave the past in the past.*

Blake was still looking at her, but he wasn't seeing her. Casually, Kaia returned the objects to her pockets since it didn't appear there was going to be any shedding of clothes in the near future.

"I do. She's up here with me."

Someone was looking for her? Surely Royce couldn't be stupid enough to draw attention to her absence, could he?

"Yeah. Hiding under the bed."

They were talking about Jo Jo.

"Tell Mrs. Nazario that I'll bring the dog down. By the way, Luke? You're in charge until I tell you otherwise." Blake tapped the earpiece. "Tina freaked out because she couldn't find Jo Jo."

When Blake said her name, the dog growled.

"Told you." Couldn't Tina have freaked out earlier? While it bolstered her story, the interruption had absolutely killed the mood. That was good, Kaia repeated to herself, and put the gloves and polishing cloth in her pocket.

Blake drew a deep breath and she felt the atmosphere

change. "Will you help me get her out from under there?" He was back to being the consummate professional, neutral tone and expression in place.

She could do professional. "Sure." Did that mean he believed her? Was she going to be able to waltz out of here with both the snuffbox and the cuffs? Best not to ask. Just assume. "Go around to the other side and grab for her so she'll scoot toward me."

"That could work." Blake got down on his hands and knees as did Kaia. "Come here, Jo Jo," he said. The dog snarled.

Kaia could learn something from Jo Jo.

She looked under the bed and saw Jo Jo backing against the wall. "She's going the wrong way."

"Jo Jo!"

"Don't yell at her! Talk baby talk like Tina does."

Blake's face appeared next to the floor, his expression disgusted. "I do not talk baby talk."

"Call her sweetums."

"No."

"Wow." Kaia looked from Jo Jo to Blake. "You never seemed like the kind of guy who'd let pride get in the way of doing his job."

Blake glared first at her, then at Jo Jo. He inhaled. "Come here, Jo Jo. *Sweetums,*" he said through gritted teeth.

Kaia giggled, tried to stop, but couldn't. "Jo…" It was all she could manage without bursting into laughter. She collapsed onto her back and laughed. It wasn't *that* funny, but she couldn't seem to stop.

"I've never heard you laugh like that before."

There hadn't been much to laugh about in a long time. Kaia turned her head and saw Blake watching her.

"You sounded scary. I wouldn't come out from under the bed, either."

"I notice she's not running to you."

Kaia patted the carpet next to her. "Come here, Jo Jo," she said, still chuckling.

"Yeah, Jo Jo. Go to Kaia." Blake reached under the bed.

Jo Jo yelped and with a surprisingly deep growl, ran at Blake, catching him off guard.

Kaia could hear the teeth snap all the way on the other side of the bed.

"Ow! She bit me and—hey!"

Kaia saw him raise his hand to his ear before Jo Jo came scrambling at her. Kaia wasn't prepared.

Jo Jo ran out from under the bed, across Kaia's stomach and out the door, which set off a fresh bout of laughter.

"Get her!" Blake yelled. "The damn dog's got my earpiece!"

Kaia found this funny, too. Laughing, she got to her feet and started for the hall after Jo Jo.

And then everything went black.

9

BLAKE WAS OUT THE door just after Kaia and at first, he thought the hall light had gone out.

"Jo Jo!" Kaia called and kept running, disappearing into the blackness.

A second later, the eerie silence registered. The power was off. *The gates.* They were up ahead but he was disoriented and didn't know how far. "Kaia, stop!"

He sprinted forward faster than he'd ever moved in his life. *"Kaia!"*

Arms outstretched, his fingers found her and grabbed hold. Yanking her to his chest, he dragged her backward as a whirring sounded and the metal security gate slammed into place.

All around them thuds and clanking sounded as the shutters closed and locked over the outside windows.

He could hear gasps and the beginning of concerned babble from the party guests in the room below.

What he didn't hear was the yelping of an annoying little dog crushed by the gate.

Heart pounding, he exhaled in relief, but he kept Kaia

clasped against his chest and tried not to visualize her pinned by the gate. She was so tiny. But not fragile.

He bent his forehead to her head. It landed in a springy knot of hair. He inhaled, but remembered that she avoided using scented products, except for the brief time she'd lived with him.

He should release her, but she wasn't pulling away, so he didn't. "That was close," he murmured into the back of her head.

"Don't you have those things on a delay?" Her voice was a little shaky and he could feel her heart beating against his arms.

"Five seconds."

"I'm glad Jo Jo had more than a five-second head start."

"Yeah. Now let's hope she doesn't choke on my earpiece."

She gave a short laugh. "Come on, Blake, say that like you mean it."

Her heart rate had slowed. His hadn't.

Back there, back in the bedroom before Luke interrupted them, Blake had been going to do something very, very dumb. He'd been going to kiss Kaia and he hadn't been going to stop until the nagging, burning, itching, craving, hungry desire he *still* felt was slaked. He'd even convinced himself she felt the same way.

She was clouding his judgment now the same way she had six years ago. If Luke's call hadn't interrupted them, who knows how far things would have gone? The way he felt about her they might have ended up naked in Tina and Casper's bed.

Inappropriate didn't begin to describe it.

But Luke's call had broken the spell and Blake was grateful. And then the lights had gone out. Blake's reaction to Kaia's near miss with the gate forced him to admit that his feelings for her went much deeper than they should. Right or wrong, they were true. So now what?

"Everyone please remain where you are," he heard Luke say to the party guests downstairs.

He tightened his arms. "You heard the man."

Kaia shushed him, but stayed where she was.

"The electricity has gone out," Luke was saying. There was some shushing from the guests. "What you heard were the security shutters closing. They're programmed to shut when the power is cut to the house. Until the power comes back on and we reset them, I ask that you all remain in this room. Other security measures are now active in the house and would cause a hazard if they were tripped."

"Do tell," Kaia murmured.

"That would spoil the surprise," Blake murmured back.

"Lasers and gas, right?" She groaned. "I *hate* lasers and gas."

"Good to know."

"Seriously, Blake, you know somebody is going to sneak away to the bathroom or Jo Jo will cross one and that gas leaves you with a hideous headache."

"Speaking from experience?"

He felt her tense. "Part of my training."

He thought about what it must have been like for her to grow up, trained from birth to steal. What kind of parents would do that to their child? "No. No gas," he told her.

She relaxed a little. "Luke's bluffing?"

"Sort of." His men would be operating by a different protocol, so it wasn't all a bluff.

"Good one."

"We're working on getting some light in here." Luke's voice rose above the crowd noise. "For your personal safety and the safety of those around you, please remain seated."

"Is it my imagination, or does he sound like a flight attendant?" Kaia asked.

"It's familiar. People respond to familiar."

"I've got loads of candles," they heard Tina say.

"Ma'am—"

There was a yelp.

"Jo Jo," he and Kaia said at the same time.

"There's Mommy's sweetums!"

Sweetums. In the dark, he felt Kaia's silent laughter and found himself smiling, too.

"I can't get a cell signal!" someone called.

An eerie blue glow became visible in the open landing on the other side of the gate as a dozen or so guests checked their cell phones. Kaia had hers out, too.

"Look." There was a "no connection" message.

"That's not good," Blake said. "If the cell towers aren't functioning, it means the outage isn't just local. Either their battery backup has failed, or they're reserving bandwidth for emergency communications."

Kaia left her cell phone screen lit and faced it forward. "You know what else isn't good?"

"Hmm?" Kaia was in his arms again and she wasn't trying to maim him. It was all good.

"We're not on the right side of the gate."

"I know."

They were standing a few feet from it because when he'd yelled for her to stop, miraculously, she had. If not…she *might* have made it through, but it would have been so close his heart was still pounding at the thought.

"You don't seem all that concerned."

"You could have been hurt." He could hear the emotion in his voice and knew she could hear it, too. He didn't care.

"But I wasn't." She patted his arm and he reluctantly let her slip away. "What are the Nazarios doing with a setup like this, anyway?"

"They host benefits and sometimes there are pieces of art here for a few days." He slowly inhaled and exhaled, striving to match her "business as usual" tone. Because for now, that was the way it had to be. "Insurance companies are limiting exposure and won't allow works to be taken to venues they consider to be at risk. If the Nazarios wanted to continue being the generous patrons of the arts that they are—"

Kaia snorted.

"That's not an attractive sound, in case no one has ever told you."

"So they upgraded. I don't need to hear how wonderful they are." She walked to the gate and examined the latches by the light of her cell phone. She tapped along the wall vertically and horizontally. "Excellent reinforcements."

"Thank you."

"Hurry up and open it." She stepped back.

Blake had wondered when they were going to get around to that. He'd been hoping the power would return before now. "I can't."

"What do you mean, you can't?" Kaia waved her arm at the latches, her phone making a glowing arc. "How are you going to reset it?"

"The office will reset the alarm code remotely when the power is restored."

"Oh, come on. You can't tell me that every time

there's a power glitch, the Nazarios are trapped in their house."

Blake avoided looking directly at the phone in her hand so his eyes would have a chance to adjust to the dark. "If the full system is turned on, then yes, they and anyone else will be trapped inside and anyone outside will not be able to get in."

"Bummer." She turned back to the locks, studying them more closely. "But I guess that's the idea."

"Right. It also means we're stuck here together." He joined her at the gate. Now that she was no longer in his arms, he felt the full impact of their situation. A high-profile job, a house full of people, his best men on duty, and Blake, himself, was AWOL. Helpless. "This is my worst nightmare," he said under his breath.

She heard. "That kind of enthusiasm could give a girl a complex."

"So could grabbing a guy by his balls."

"I thought you were over that."

"You told me not to forget, not that there's any chance," he snapped, increasingly frustrated at being unable to join his team below.

"I didn't expect you to keep bringing it up."

"No? How do your victims usually act?"

"They're very polite. Much politer than you." She started walking back toward the bedroom wing, taking the light with her.

"Where are you going?"

"In search of better company," she called over her shoulder.

He was being a jerk. "Kaia—wait. I'm angry and frustrated and I'm taking it out on you. The power failure is not your fault. Is it?" he asked, trying for a little humor.

"I'm flattered you think so highly of my capabilities." She slowly returned. "But no. And it's not your fault, either."

"Doesn't matter. Not only are the Nazarios my biggest clients, I have other clients in the crowd downstairs. And now they get to see me in action. Or inaction, as it happens." He laced his fingers through the gate's diamond patterned grid and stared through it toward the hall's open area.

Shadows flickered, punctuated by flashlight beams. He could hear Luke directing the men to bring chairs into the room. There was chatter, but not panic. So far.

"Sounds to me as though Luke is doing okay by himself," Kaia said.

"It's not Luke's company."

Kaia turned around and leaned against the gate while looking down at her phone. "Still no signal." She turned off the screen and darkness swallowed them. "You don't have an override code? A panic key?"

"No." Blake gave the gate an impotent shake. "I don't recommend them. If all thieves knew there were panic keys, they could force owners to override their own systems."

He stared toward her, wishing he could read her expression. Was he telling her something she already knew?

"You're staring at me," she said.

"How do you know?"

"I can feel you."

He laughed.

"You're wondering if we ever forced a mark to use a panic key."

"Yes," he admitted after a beat.

"No." She turned and faced the gate. "There's no

skill involved in that. We were burglars, not robbers."
Her tone said that robbers were the scum of the earth.

He found that oddly reassuring. Why, he had no idea.
In the end, it was theft either way.

"So aren't you going to let your men know we're up
here?" she asked. "The balcony isn't that far away. If
we both yelled, they could hear us easy."

And how great would it look that Blake had been
trapped by his own security system? He shook his head.
"No." Maybe the power outage wouldn't last long and no
one would have to know they'd been trapped. "They've
got enough to do keeping the guests from panicking."

A yellowish glint shone in her eyes, a reflection of
the wobbling yellow candlelight that had joined the blue
cell phone glow from downstairs. She moved away.

"*Now* where are you going?"

"Over here."

He strained to see and made out her arms and shoulders sliding down the wall. "What are you doing?"

"I'm sitting for my personal safety and the safety of
those around me. Come on, Blake. Just chill, okay?"

He remained where he was. "I should be down there."
And he would have been, if he hadn't been so focused
on Kaia.

"So should I. Royce must be *freaking.*"

"We'll do an inventory before we allow anyone to
leave."

"*That'll* be real popular."

"Yeah." Blake exhaled. "I'm not looking forward to
implying Tina's staff and guests can't be trusted."

"You've tagged everybody, Blake. I think that ship
has sailed."

"Maybe so. But it was for their safety, too. Kidnap-
ping. Hostages. You know."

"Uh, no. I don't know. Wow. You're either paranoid or very thorough."

"Both." He stared at the flickering light. It was brighter now, enough to make out the walls and the railing on the landing. "I hope Royce has already started packing the jewelry away."

"Are you kidding?" Kaia asked. "He's got a captive audience and the romance of candlelight. He's in seller's heaven."

"Where's the music?" Tina's loud voice carried easily from below. "Let's have some music!"

"No amps," someone replied. Probably one of the musicians.

"You don't need amps!" Tina called out. "Just play louder!"

"Can't see," another complained.

"Oh, for pity's sake. Half the time you've got your eyes shut anyway because you're making stuff up as you go along!"

That drew a couple of chuckles. The bass player started plunking and some anemic jazz followed.

"People, this is like one, great, big ole slumber party!" Tina shouted. "Whoo! Keep those drinks a' comin'!"

"Oh, great." Blake stalked over and sat next to Kaia. "Alcohol and candles. Wonderful combination."

He saw her look at the ceiling. "It would be reee-aaallly bad if the sprinklers were set off, wouldn't it?"

Blake groaned.

"Millions of dollars in artwork ruined."

"Kaia…"

"Just saying."

Blake stared at her uneasily, trying to read her

expression. Not that he could ever read it, even in bright light, if she didn't want him to.

"You just can't trust me, can you?" she asked.

Blake was silent.

"Did I say anything you weren't thinking?"

"It was the way you said it."

"Because I wouldn't be sad for Casper and his wife? I'd be sad for the loss of the art. I'd even be sad for the insurance company. Somebody downstairs would be guaranteed to slip and fall and I'd be sad about that. But Casper and Tina?" She made a derisive sound. "They don't deserve what they've got."

"Is that how you justified stealing from them?"

The air seemed to freeze as Kaia slowly turned her head and faced him. "I stole nothing."

She was facing the landing and he could make out her expression, thanks to the candles and her pale skin. But it was the tone in her voice that caught him. "I'm supposed to believe Casper Nazario gave you that diamond necklace."

"Why do you believe he didn't?"

"Because—" Blake broke off.

"Because that's what he said," Kaia echoed his thoughts. "And the word of a rich, powerful man with a smart lawyer is worth more than a nineteen-year-old college girl with a public defender."

"But—"

"You knew me, Blake. You didn't know him and yet you believed him instead of me."

She was right. "I was given the case."

"To investigate? Or had you already made up your mind?"

His mind had been made up for him. And he hadn't

been investigating; he'd been supposed to get close to her so they could get to family.

As he stared at her in the dim light, her expression softened and he was facing the young woman he'd known. "I never lied to you," she said.

In that moment, everything that had made Blake a talented police detective told him she was telling the truth. He felt it in his gut.

He thought his instincts had let him down with Kaia, but that had been because he'd been told she was lying, that she'd stolen a diamond pendant. She'd worn the thing around her neck and told him it was a gift, which was so unbelievable, she'd almost convinced him it was true. It *felt* true. So when he caught himself doubting his superiors, he figured she was the most dangerously, clever liar he'd ever come across.

But she hadn't been lying. His instincts *hadn't* let him down. The whole premise of the case had been wrong.

At the realization, something within him settled and calmed. It was as though he'd been trying to see through a snowstorm and it was now the morning after with the sun shining and the air clear and still.

But he was going to have to deal with the snow.

One of the lieutenants he'd worked with on the force had a saying, "When the puzzle pieces don't fit, try a different puzzle."

Blake had blamed faulty judgment, beat himself up over getting emotionally involved with a criminal and had quit police work because he'd thought he'd gone soft. The case against Kaia had never felt *right* to him, the pieces hadn't fit, and he'd never been able to put it out of his mind. If she was telling the truth, then Casper had lied and Blake was looking at a different puzzle.

Kaia was innocent. He made himself think it, even

though it meant he'd made the mistake every officer wants to avoid.

He studied her, mentally working out the new puzzle. "You had the diamond."

"Casper *gave* it to me."

It's what she'd said all along. "Why?"

"You read my statement," she said with weary resignation.

"Tell me anyway. I need to hear you say the words." They'd never discussed the details; he'd only read them.

"Will it make a difference?"

He started to demand, to raise his voice, but what came out of his mouth was a whispered, "Please. For me."

It surprised both of them.

"Okay." Looping her arms around her raised knees, she leaned against the wall. "I did some work for Casper." She stared straight ahead instead of at Blake, but he didn't need to see her expression. He'd be able to hear the truth in her voice.

"You're all worried about me being around jewelry when you should be worried about Tina." Kaia glanced at him. "She's a kleptomaniac. She's the one with the problem." She turned away. "And Casper knows."

Interesting. Blake mentally filed the info. "How did you get involved with him?"

"Royce. He used to work for my dad."

"I thought—"

"Designing and repairing jewelry! Jeez! He's totally legit, or he has been for years, so don't go there."

Blake held up a hand. "Not going there."

"Casper's weasel of a lawyer was sniffing around because Tina's souvenir gathering was getting out of control. Their friends were getting suspicious, so Casper got the bright idea of putting the missing things back so they'd be found and there'd be a lot of 'Oh, how did that get there?' and 'I've been looking for that!' and my personal fav 'the maid must have knocked it off the shelf.'"

"So you're saying Casper hired you to break into houses and put back the items Tina had stolen." And she hadn't seen a problem with that?

"Yes." She nodded. "Four houses and one office. I put some guy's grandfather's service medal into a brief-case."

"And Casper paid you with the diamond?"

"No, in cash—that's how I got the money for school. Where we met." She bit off the words. "Giving me the diamond was an impulse. He'd seen me looking at it and he was so relieved that I'd returned everything without anyone knowing, that he gave it to me. 'A cat's eye for a cat burglar' he'd said."

"It was a generous impulse," Blake said, deliberately neutral. The thing was worth thousands and the Casper he knew was not impulsive.

"I figured it was like a tip, you know?"

"That's quite a tip."

"Not when you consider what was at stake for him. And I knew he'd need me again so I figured that was part of it, too. Kind of like a retainer. In fact—" Blake saw her shift. "...these cuffs?" She held up one of the silver and turquoise bracelets. The silver caught the ambient light and glowed. "Tina walked off with them after that exhibit I told you about. Casper usually pays the invoices when she 'borrows' from designers and stores, but these aren't for sale." She turned the cuff over in her hands. "Something to do with Royce's family history, so he wants them back. Whatever. Casper went looking for them and lo and behold, discovered that Tina's installed new hiding places. He hired me to retrieve these and tell him what else I found."

"You mean, after he sent you to prison, he had the nerve to contact you? And you agreed? Are you insane?"

Her mouth twisted. "He met my price."

"And what was that?"

"A lot of money. There aren't many job opportunities for an ex-con with my skills." She put the cuff on her wrist and twisted it, admiring the silver in the dim light. "And I wanted to get these back for Royce."

Blake could accept that, although if it were him, he'd use this opportunity for revenge. "Why didn't Casper just get the bracelets himself?"

"He doesn't have the combination to Tina's safes— I found two, but there might be more. And here's the kicker—he doesn't want Tina to know he's aware of her problem."

No way. And yet Blake could believe it. "That's…"

"Sick?" Kaia supplied.

"I was going for unrealistic."

"But sick works."

It sure did. "Casper has to know that Tina knows he's ignoring her kleptomania."

"Duh. I'm thinking that's why she got her own safes."

That Blake hadn't installed. "You say Tina's been stealing for years?"

"Apparently."

Wonderful. His most important client was a compulsive thief. "Eventually she'll get caught. Why doesn't Casper deal with it and get her some help?"

Kaia gave a derisive laugh. "You've seen Tina and you've seen Casper. Why do you think?"

An image of the voluptuous Tina and her much older husband appeared in Blake's mind. "He's been covering for her all these years because he's afraid she'll leave him if he confronts her?"

"That would be my guess."

And there was the missing gold-plated puzzle piece: Casper's motivation. Unreal. How could a powerful and ruthless businessman have such an obvious weakness?

Kaia was watching him, reading his expression. Blake suspected she could see in the dark a lot better than he could.

"What I don't understand is why he reported the diamond stolen," he said. "You could have blackmailed Tina."

"He knew nobody would believe me. You didn't. The police didn't. As far as they were concerned, I was confessing to multiple burglaries."

Casper had been ruthlessly clever. He'd duped the police and he'd duped Blake. He'd set up Kaia—maybe that had been his plan from the start. "After what he did to you, how could any amount of money be enough to work for the man again?"

"I had no choice." Kaia blew out a breath. "Terms of my probation. This time, though, the weasel knows, my lawyer knows, Royce knows, Casper knows—and now you know. Tina doesn't know, but she claims she already returned the cuffs, so if you tell her I've got them, what's she going to say? You ought to see the junk she's stolen. She's probably forgotten all about these."

Blake was reeling. Casper had said nothing to him, yet had authorized what was essentially an attempted theft on Blake's watch. Or an actual theft, since Kaia had the cuffs. *What are you up to, old man?*

"Why didn't you tell me this when we were in the

bedroom?" he demanded. "One call, and I could have verified your story."

"Confidentiality clause. That I've just broken." She shifted and he guessed she was putting the cuffs away. "If you say anything, I'll claim the blackout as extenuating circumstances."

Blake was convinced that not only was this story legit; Kaia had been telling the truth all along. Casper had lied and sent her to prison. *Casper had lied to Blake.* Anger welled within him. He was going to make this right. Somehow. "I won't say anything to anyone. I swear I won't."

He felt her gaze on him, could see the gleam in her unblinking eyes. "You believe me?"

Blake swallowed hard against a knot of anger and regret. "Yes." His voice was rough.

He reached for her, wrapping his arms around her. He needed to hold Kaia, but her body was stiff. Blake didn't blame her. Right now, he hated himself, too.

"Part of me believed you before, but I told myself I'd lost my objectivity instead of trusting my instincts. I'm sorry." He rubbed his hand across her unyielding back. "So very sorry."

She didn't move away, but she didn't relax, either.

His fingers caught the edges of her shoulder blades and skimmed the muscles above them. They weren't as developed as they'd been, but her upper body still had a gymnast's shape. She was exercising, but she wasn't training and he remembered that when they'd met, she'd been trying for a gymnastic scholarship.

She'd lost that opportunity, too.

He wanted to make it up to her. He wanted to make up everything to her.

"You lied to me," she said. "Our whole relationship was a lie."

Blake squeezed his eyes shut. Yeah, first they had to get past some stuff. "It was my job."

She pushed out of his arms. "And you did it *really* well." What he could see of her expression was blank, but the rapid rise and fall of her shoulders as she breathed gave away her agitation.

"You must hate me."

"I should!" She waited several beats. "I *want* to." With a disgusted sound, she turned away. "But I don't. I can't."

Relief made him release the breath he hadn't known he was holding. "Good. Because our relationship may have started out that way, but there was a lot of truth to it."

She turned her head warily. "What part?"

Blake took her hand. Her fingers were curled into a fist. Gently, he loosened them. "This part." He pressed her palm against his chest, above his heart.

She stared at her hand. "I can feel your heart racing."

"It's this way every time I'm with you," he told her. "When I touch you. When you touch me. When I *think* about touching you. And only you."

Seconds went by.

"Arresting you tore me up. I studied the paperwork, tried to get them to reexamine the case until I was put on indefinite leave. But your background and the other burglaries…I'm sorry."

"Blake," she whispered, finally.

And it seemed like the most natural thing in the world for her to lean forward and for Blake to bring his mouth to hers.

He wanted the kiss to be a tender apology, sweet and

giving. Soft. Gentle. All about showing Kaia he'd had genuine feelings for her. *Still* had genuine feelings for her.

He'd hurt her and he'd hurt himself and he wanted her to know that. He wasn't going to ask for her to kiss him back, but wasn't going to object if she did.

Above all, he would not lose control. He'd remain aware of her body language and at the first tensing, the first tug backward, he'd release her. He had no right to expect her to forgive him, especially when he hadn't yet forgiven himself.

But with the first touch of her mouth, desire raged in spite of all his good intentions. It was as though knowing the truth had removed what little restraint he'd had. He wanted to part her lips and tangle his tongue with hers. And he wanted her to kiss him back with the passion she'd shown six years ago.

But how could she?

So much had happened. So much betrayal and hurt. Not hating him was a long way from wanting him. Loving him.

If he wanted another chance with Kaia, he'd need patience, lots of patience. And he'd give her time, all she needed. And space. But not too much space.

Blake held himself with an iron control as he softly kissed her, daring to touch her lower lip with the tip of his tongue only once because the wave of longing he felt made him clench his fingers against her back.

Kaia's hand was still pressed against his chest. She slipped it from between them and Blake prepared to pull away. But instead of withdrawing, Kaia slid her hand around his neck to the back of his head and urged him closer.

Her mouth opened beneath his.

She was kissing him back.

After everything that had happened, *she was kissing him back.*

His tongue met hers and Blake went a little dizzy. Maybe a lot dizzy. His pulse pounded and desire flooded his senses. He couldn't think straight when she was in his arms. He didn't *want* to think straight. He wanted to let go and just feel. The truth was that this was the first time he'd felt right since that horrible night in the mall parking lot.

Blake hauled her into his lap so her legs draped over his thighs, desperate to have as much of his body in contact with as much of hers as he could. His elbow banged against the gate, momentarily reminding him of where they were, but he didn't care.

That was the power she had over him.

She could have asked him to do anything for her and he would have agreed. The feeling was devastatingly familiar.

This time, instead of panicking, he kissed her harder. He kissed her until his lips went numb, also a familiar feeling.

Wrenching his mouth from hers, he pressed kisses along her throat, gently sucking at the steady pulse in her neck.

"Blake!" Kaia pushed his mouth away. "I'm supposed to be modeling necklaces!"

"Sorry," he muttered, not sorry. "I wasn't thinking."

"And I like that about you," she said, her voice breathy. "You were always totally in the moment, completely with me."

He raised his head. "Why would I want to be anywhere else?"

Kaia smiled and his lips tingled.

She wiggled in his lap and his lips weren't all that tingled. "I want to be completely with you some more," he added.

She lifted her chin. "Then kiss me again."

And this time, I won't let you go, Blake vowed as he lowered his mouth. He wanted to say it aloud, but it was too soon for her. So for now, he'd cherish her and give her such pleasure that she wouldn't *want* to leave.

10

Kiss me again. What was she thinking? Where was this headed? She should never have kissed him back because now she didn't want to stop.

Kaia hadn't let any man get close to her since Blake. She didn't trust men. She didn't trust herself. With good reason, if the way she felt now was any indication. She remembered this gnawing craving to be close, as though nothing less than climbing into his skin would be enough.

Good and bad memories of him warred within her. She would not, *not* weaken, not give in. Wanting to know if any part of what they'd had together had been real was dumb and self-indulgent. His kisses were distracting her from her purpose for being here tonight. She had a lot at stake and she wasn't going to throw away a better future for momentary pleasure.

Truth or lies didn't matter any more. The past couldn't change.

Sure, Blake had said all the right things—well some of them, anyway. And she'd told him as much of the truth now as she dared, which was everything except about the snuffbox.

Lies were still between them, only this time, they were hers. How ironic.

"No other woman makes me feel the way you do," he murmured against her mouth. "That's why I quit the force."

"You quit because of me?" She was stunned.

"When you go undercover, you've got to be able to trust your gut and mine was all twisted. You got to me then and you're getting to me now."

Kaia was helplessly aware of her frozen emotions thawing and about to flood her sense of self-preservation. She wanted to believe him; of course she wanted to believe him. What woman wouldn't want to think she had that kind of power over a man?

Her heart thudded wildly as the little voice inside her insisted he could be lying now. He could be telling her what he thought she wanted to hear. And he'd be right—it was exactly what she wanted to hear. She hated that. Now, this very moment, he could be kissing her with lying lips and caressing her with lying hands.

She was wrong, all wrong. The truth did matter. It shouldn't, but it did.

Kaia drew back to clear her head. "You're admitting that I get to you? Aren't you afraid I'll use it against you?" She was crazy to point that out.

"Absolutely." He gave her a crooked smile that charmed its way into her heart.

But her heart was smarter this time around. Wasn't it? "So now what?"

He leaned down until his mouth was positioned a breath away from hers. "Now you kiss me."

She swayed toward him in spite of herself. "Why?"

"Because you want to." His fingers spanned her shoulders and his thumb ran beneath her collarbone. "And I want you to."

Kaia shivered. "Why?" she asked again, mostly to stall for time. Her original idea had been to seduce *him,* to let him think he could manipulate her the way he had before, not to actually *let* him manipulate her.

Not such a great idea after all.

Especially since she wasn't sure who was doing the manipulating. Was he telling the truth? Or was he lying the way he had before?

Kaia had a headache. And aches in other places.

"You can tell a lot from a kiss," Blake murmured.

Kaia certainly hoped so. "Especially if you kiss a lot."

Blake touched his forehead to hers. "Wanna test your theory?" He stole a butterfly kiss.

Kaia laughed, suddenly feeling happy for no good reason. And then she kissed him, also for no good reason, fitting her lips to his as though time hadn't passed and he hadn't betrayed her.

Warmth, a sense of relief, and a lot of other complicated emotions she didn't want to uncomplicate just then flowed through her. When Blake cradled her next to his body, it just felt right. As simple and as complex as that.

This, this was what a kiss was supposed to feel like. No anger. A soft promise of later passion. As though they had all the time in the world. As though they were the only two people in the world.

It was...nice. Kaia hadn't experienced nice a whole lot in her life. At the moment, nice had more power over her than passion and that was dangerous. She drew back.

"That wasn't much of a kiss," he echoed her earlier taunt.

"This will be," she quoted his reply. *Because passion will be safer than tenderness.*

Then her mouth was on his and she was kissing Blake, really, seriously kissing him after six long, long years, and all her hate and resentment was melting away when she wanted to keep it wrapped around her for protection.

She pitied women who did dumb things because of the way a man made them feel. Now she pitied herself as longing swept through her and she knew she was going to do something stupid before the night was over. Clearly, passion wasn't any safer than nice.

But speaking of nice… Blake's mouth was hot and sweet and addictive. In seconds Kaia was back to those days when they'd kissed for so long, her lips had gone numb. Her body continued warming and thawing as though a long winter had ended. She couldn't stop wanting him, even though she'd regret it.

She explored his mouth and invited him to explore hers, and then realized it was more about remembering the taste and scent of their mingled breaths than discovering something new.

Blake made a low sound in the back of his throat and deepened the kiss because she'd pressed herself as close as she could get to him. She could feel the heat of his body through his shirt and suit jacket. Burrowing her hands beneath the fabric was like sticking them into an oven. His shirt had gone damp and limp, like her willpower.

It was the touching that was her weakness. Kaia had been raised as a loner and her parents weren't the demonstrative types. There hadn't been a lot of hugging or loving touches. Hugging was for picking pockets.

She'd been a surprise to them, especially to her father who was in his forties when she'd been conceived. Her mother was younger by ten years. Maybe more, maybe less. She'd always been vague about her age. Kaia hadn't felt unloved, exactly, but she'd sensed she'd been a bother until her father had discovered her gymnastic talent. That coupled with her tiny hands and uncanny ability to assess jewels had made him a much more enthusiastic parent. As long as Kaia performed. Perfectly.

Kaia felt Blake's hands on her shoulders, skimming down her arms and back up again, caressing her skin. He'd liked her soft skin, she remembered. And she liked having him touch it. With her parents, any touch was light, if she felt it at all, and it meant they were lifting something from a pocket or a purse. Testing her. They'd trained her never to relax. Never let her guard down. Never trust anyone.

And so she hadn't, until Blake.

When he caressed her, it was because he found pleasure in it and wanted to give pleasure to her. And he did. He *so* did.

Kaia sighed into his mouth as his hand left her arm and circled her waist, drawing her closer to his chest. She'd never had enough of the pleasure, the closeness.

They'd spent their few precious Sunday afternoons together sitting this way with Kaia in his lap, her legs draped over his, doing her class work while Blake watched some football game on TV, the sound muted in consideration for her.

They kissed during commercials.

And sometimes more.

She'd had no idea there were so many long commercials during football games.

Kaia withdrew her hand from beneath his jacket and traced his jaw with her fingertips, circling his ear. The sharp edge of his fresh haircut prickled softly the way she remembered. He felt the same and with her eyes closed, she could imagine that it was the same.

Except it wasn't. "Blake—"

She forgot what she was going to ask because his hand left her waist and slowly skimmed upward. She tensed in anticipation, biting her lower lip, wondering if he would stop, equally hoping he would and hoping he wouldn't, until his hand closed over her breast.

She inhaled at the sharp pleasure, wishing it didn't feel *quite* so good.

"Blake," she breathed and this time, she wasn't thinking of anything else as she tilted her head back.

He kissed her jaw, the side of her neck, and her throat. "Your skin is still so soft, so smooth."

"And your beard is still rough."

He raised his head. "I used to shave three times a day because I couldn't stand seeing the red marks I left."

"Didn't work."

"No. I couldn't stay away from you." He kneaded her breast, his thumb maddeningly skimming the edge of her neckline. "I can't stay away from you now."

"I'm not going anywhere," she heard herself tell him, even though she should get to her feet, run down the hall, grab a set of free weights, smash the sauna window and make her escape.

But then she'd have to stop his fingers from toying with her neckline…slipping beneath

She drew a shuddering breath and wiggled against the bulge in his lap. He wanted her. She wanted him.

It was decision time. Either she was going to end this now—gently, but firmly. In a classy way and not a pathetic, whiny, clingy way.

Or she was not.

And if she was not, then she wasn't going to stick her toe into the water; she was going to jump in and make a big splash, hollering the whole time.

Blake nuzzled the side of her neck, her collarbone, and traced his tongue in the hollow there as his thumb dipped beneath her neckline to the strapless bra she wore. Involuntarily, her back arched so much she was nearly bent in two.

Time to jump and make a big splash. Kaia pushed away Blake's hands, but that was only so she could peel down her dress and bra.

Calling a halt, classy or otherwise, was no longer an option.

He murmured something. She didn't know or care what.

"Touch me," she whispered, hoping it didn't sound as if she was begging.

And he did, murmuring, "So beautiful," with his mouth against her breast.

Kaia laughed a little wildly. "You can't see anything."

Blake ran his hands over her bare skin. "I can feel and I can remember."

Kaia's breath hitched as she felt and remembered, too. Because really, that was what this was about. A last time together to remember the good and erase what came after. Kaia wanted to re-create the intense emotional and physical connection with Blake that she'd never had with anyone else. Or if it was broken, then she wanted to know that, too.

The world they'd created now could only live in the

dark. Once the lights came back on, they'd return to their real lives.

Kaia had always preferred the dark. She placed a hand on either side of his face and kissed him lightly before winding her arms around his neck.

Blake cupped her breasts. Drawing one tip into his mouth, he rubbed his thumb across the other, sending a hot zing straight to her middle.

She gasped as her muscles jerked. She was so used to training and exercising to maintain perfect control over her body that when it reacted without any effort on her part, she was caught unaware. For some reason, she'd thought she'd be able to control whether or not she felt anything with Blake this time. But her body remembered and was participating whether she wanted to or not.

Of course she *wanted* to, but the more she enjoyed herself, the harder it would be to walk away later. This had better be worth it.

Blake must have been able to read her mind. His tongue swirled over her with *just* the right speed and *just* the right pressure. Kaia quivered and flexed and bit her lip as a low moan escaped. The back of his neck felt like iron and she realized he was supporting all her weight the way she was hanging off him. She shifted one hand to his shoulder and burrowed the other beneath his jacket as it covered her like a tent.

She was surrounded by his scent and inhaled deeply. She'd remember this combination of soap and man forever.

Blake's breath was hot and when he moved from one breast to the other, Kaia barely felt the coolness on her damp skin.

No power, she recalled. No air conditioning. No way to open the windows. A room full of people. Heat rises.

Beneath the suit jacket, she was becoming uncomfortably warm. Blake must be burning up. She ran her hand over his back. His shirt was seriously damp. "It's so hot!"

"Oh, yeah," he mumbled around her breast.

She chuckled. "I meant temperature."

"Is it?"

Kaia worked the jacket off his shoulders. Blake raised his head long enough to shrug out of it.

"Uhm, maybe the gun and holster, too?" she asked.

"Were you always this picky?" His teeth gleamed and she knew he was grinning.

"I have standards," she said, as she loosened his tie.

"Hmm." Blake dropped the gun and ran his hands up her thighs.

Kaia stilled instantly as his palms bumped over the cuffs in her hidden pockets and the tools beneath her leggings. She'd been so caught up in memories and feelings, she'd forgotten. *Forgotten.* If he'd started running his hands at her calf instead of her thigh, he would have discovered the snuffbox, not that he would have known what it was. But it might have stopped him. He might have asked. And she'd have had to tell him.

How could she have lost her mind like that?

But she always lost her good sense around Blake. She ditched reality and entered her own little world with him. It had got her into trouble then and was about to get her into trouble now.

He was laughing lightly, but her heart pounded. "You travel with a lot of baggage."

Baggage she didn't want to show him if she didn't

have to. She tried to sound sexy. "Well, you know me and pockets."

"I do." He leaned back and shadows flickered behind him. "Are you going to finish taking off my tie? Or..." He moved suggestively in time to the jazzy beat in the background. Taking over the task, he slowly loosened his tie, drew it from around his neck and then twirled it over his head, making Kaia laugh before he tossed it toward the discarded suit jacket.

Then, still moving in time to the music, he started unbuttoning his shirt. "Feel free to join in."

Kaia gestured to her naked torso. The top part of her dress was scrunched at her waist. "I have a head start."

He suddenly stopped unbuttoning his shirt and pulled it over his head in a single motion. "Now I've caught up."

"So you have." Obviously, Blake wasn't thinking about Kaia's pockets or what might be in them and she wanted to keep it that way. She splayed both hands on his chest, tracing his muscles and skimming over his ribs. He was more muscular than before and he'd been no couch potato then. "Bulking up?"

"Not as much as when I first started out on my own. People like their security escorts with big shoulders."

Kaia nodded, thinking of Tyrone and his big shoulders, that made her think of Blake's men and *their* big shoulders and that they might come looking for him at any moment.

Kaia glanced down the hallway. Due to the dim light, they would see anyone who came up the stairs before being seen—if they were paying attention.

That was highly unlikely since Blake chose that moment to take her hands and loop them around his neck before distracting her with a thorough kiss.

Kaia immediately lost herself in his kiss. It had been so long since she'd been able to completely lose herself in a kiss. Not since Blake. Loneliness had driven her to make the attempt, but she'd always remained detached, wary, and watching. Being with another man had never felt right. But then being with Blake had felt right and that turned out to be wrong.

She was going to stop thinking now, which was a good decision because Blake's deep, drugging kisses made it impossible.

Kaia ran her hands over the taut skin of his back, reacquainting herself with the play of hard muscles and the indentation beneath one of his ribs where he'd caught the edge of a table in a fight. She moved her mouth away and pressed their naked torsos together, craving the feel of skin on skin. She enjoyed being surrounded by a man's body, this man's anyway.

"You always were a burrower," Blake murmured against her ear.

"I like being touched," she confessed.

"And I like touching you." His hand was lightly moving up and down in the small of her back. "I like the feel of your skin." He moved his hand up her arm. "I like how strong you are." Skimming her shoulder, he fanned his fingers over the side of her neck. "I like feeling how fast your pulse is beating and knowing that you look so cool on the outside, but you're wild for me on the inside."

"Not cool on the outside." Kaia pulled back reluctantly as she felt a drop of sweat trickle in the valley between her breasts.

Blake took advantage. "And I *love* touching you here." He cupped her breast and rubbed his thumb across her nipple.

Kaia caught her lip between her teeth as she felt a warm tug deep in her stomach. Yes, she was pretty much all thawed out now.

Blake's mouth took over from his hand and he licked and swirled and sucked while Kaia wiggled and squirmed and clutched at his iron-hard shoulders.

She needed more, she *wanted* more, but Blake persisted in his maddeningly slow attentions.

At one point, a frustrated Kaia actually balled her fist and smacked him on that iron-hard shoulder. It had no effect whatsoever. He was holding himself back, she realized. That's why his arms were hard and the cords in his neck stood out and there was the slightest quiver of straining muscles. He wasn't allowing himself to feel the passion that wracked her body, probably out of a misguided sense of nobility. She didn't want nobility; she wanted him incoherent with desire and kissing her hard wherever his mouth landed and not thinking about it so much. "Blake!" She meant to be demanding, but it sounded too much like a sob.

He blew across her breasts, raising gooseflesh. "Better?"

"Yes, but no." Kaia drew a trembling breath. "I want you with me."

She leaned forward and licked Blake's neck, kissing her way to the spot just above his heart. She stopped there and traced a heart shape with her tongue.

She hadn't intended to. It was something she used to do, telling him she loved him without saying the words. She'd never told him that's what it meant or that it was a heart.

She'd loved the person he was pretending to be, not the real person.

"Oh, Kaia. I've missed you. I've missed this."

He bent his knees that caused her to roll against his naked chest and it felt so good, she wanted to weep. Then he started playing with her breasts again and it felt even better. It felt real.

She lifted her mouth to his, nipping at his lip as she wiggled back and forth over the hard length in his pants, finding just the right spot. Finding the right spot used to be easier, back when they sat on the couch, but she'd been wearing less clothing then.

"Let me." Blake's hand skimmed beneath her dress.

As soon as his fingers touched the edge of her leggings, Kaia jumped as though she'd been burned.

"Kaia?" Blake withdrew his hand. "I thought…" The breath whistled through his teeth. "I'm making some serious assumptions when I have no right to."

"No!" She touched his arm as he leaned back. "It's just…" *It's just that I didn't tell you about my little side job, the one that affects my future, and possibly world peace.*

As good as they were together physically, if the electricity hadn't gone out and they hadn't been trapped, Blake would never have listened to her version of what happened six years ago. At the moment, he seemed to believe her and to trust her, but when the lights came back on, would he still?

She couldn't take the chance that he wouldn't. She was going to have to keep him from discovering the snuffbox and exactly what she was wearing beneath her dress.

"You didn't misread the signals," she told him. "But…while we can't get completely carried away…" She gave him a sexy smile and put her hand on his thigh. "There are still a lot of things we can do."

Blake stared at her for a moment. *"Oh."* He exhaled and relaxed. "You're worried about a condom."

Well, no, but she should have been. Anyway, it was the perfect excuse. "I've got a lot of stuff in my pockets, but not one of those. But I don't think you'll mind too much." She reached for his zipper.

This time, Blake flinched, which she should have expected.

"I wasn't—"

"I know. That was just reflex. Anyway, I'm prepared." He started pawing through his jacket.

What? "You are?"

There was a click followed by a beam of bluish light. "Yeah. I'm a regular Boy Scout."

The flashlight showed the face of a man on a mission. Kaia used to stare at him when he slept and now noted subtle changes. His face had matured; his cheekbones were more pronounced and his jaw was fuller. The shadows emphasized a line or two at the corners of his eyes that probably weren't visible in normal lighting. There was nothing that said "boy" about him.

"Boy Scout. That's not exactly the way I think of you," she said.

He laughed softly. "I'm talking about the 'be prepared' part."

"I got that." He had a condom? Talk about mixed emotions. On one hand, yippee, but on the other, getting out of her leggings without him noticing all the stuff she had secreted beneath her dress was going to be problematic, not to mention a mood killer.

On yet another hand, there was a lot to be said for being highly motivated. And it *was* dark. The dim light created interesting shadows on his sculpted torso and Kaia decided that she was very highly motivated.

Blake unzipped a flat pouch about the size of a paperback. "Standard TransSecure issue. All my men carry them. You wouldn't believe what security escorts and bodyguards get asked for, especially when a limo is involved."

He shined the flashlight on the open pouch and Kaia saw tape, safety pins, a tiny mending kit with scissors, bandages, aspirin, hand sanitizer, wipes, tissues, transit way tokens, a comb, mirror, lip balm, breath mints, antacids, and, yes, condoms. Multiple brands. Flavored and unflavored.

"Wow." She could be motivated for a very long time with that stash.

"I would have said something earlier, but I didn't think we were there yet. Come on." He nudged her off his lap. "Let's go find a bedroom and get naked."

"Wait." Kaia thought quickly. Darkness was her friend. Although he was currently distracted, once the lights came back on, Blake would notice things Kaia didn't want him noticing, like her thick leggings. Right now, if he'd even noticed, he probably assumed they were some type of underwear, and she wanted to keep it that way.

"I don't want to wait." Blake's voice sounded thick and single-minded.

"Neither do I," Kaia said. "That's my point." She got on all fours and crawled toward him. "We don't need a bedroom."

His eyes widened. "You mean…here?"

She nodded.

"Now?"

"Umm hmm."

She could see the glint in his eyes and watched it

shift as he glanced down the hall. "Someone might come up the stairs."

"I know." He'd be thinking about being caught and about the sex and he wouldn't have the brain cells left to think about anything else. "It kind of turns me on."

"*Does* it." His voice took on an entirely different tone and Kaia discovered that it *did* kind of turn her on.

She stood on her knees and extended her right leg into the shadows. Blake looked down the hallway once more, his head tilted as he listened to the crowd noise and music, assessing and analyzing. Calculating the odds of someone searching for them.

Not focused on her. Yet.

Kaia reached beneath her dress and peeled off one legging and an elastic band filled with bits of metal picks and wires that was stuck to her thigh. She hid the soft ripping sound in the rustle of fabric and straddled his legs, arranging the folds of her dress to cushion the contents of her hidden pockets.

Blake looked up at her. "Are we really going to do this?"

"Yes." She could hardly believe it herself. Blindly, she grabbed a packet from the pouch and tossed it to him. "Yes, we are." And once more, she reached for his zipper.

His hand clamped around her wrist. "Not so fast."

Kaia felt as if her heart jumped to her throat. Did he suspect something? Had she been too aggressive? They'd never done anything like this before and she was no exhibitionist. In fact, she'd spent her life trying to blend in.

But Blake turned her wrist until her palm was face up and kissed it. His hair brushed against her nipples and she twitched.

He smiled up at her as he released her hand. "If we're going to do this, we're going to enjoy ourselves." Slowly, he moved his hand under her hitched-up skirt and skimmed it up her bare leg.

Her heart pounded and she went all liquid inside. As his hand crept along the soft flesh of her inner thigh, she felt her nerves tighten in anticipation. She was ready for this. She was ready for pretty much anything.

Kaia clutched at his shoulders, tugging him toward her, but he held himself away and instead of moving faster, his hand slowed, the pressure somewhere between a tickle and a caress. She rocked toward him and he immediately stopped.

"Hold still."

Was he kidding? "I...don't want to."

"I know." And he waited.

Why? She could hardly stand it. Suddenly, she lunged for him, hoping he'd stop playing and give in to raw desire, but he leaned out of reach. "Don't. Move."

Don't move? *Don't move?* Was he kidding? She pressed his hand against her thigh and tugged upward, but he resisted. And then he slid in the wrong direction.

Okay, *fine.* Making a frustrated sound, Kaia clamped her legs on either side of his, but her muscles betrayed her with a tremble. "I can't!"

She felt his smile. "Good."

"Blake!" she wailed.

He inched upward.

Kaia moved before she could stop herself and again, he stopped. "Why are you doing this?" she moaned.

"The slower the burn, the hotter the fire, and the bigger the explosion."

"Unless the fuse goes out."

"I'll light it again." But he moved faster, his fingers lightly stroking from side to side.

Kaia felt her skin prickle from the inside out. She felt both hot and cold at the same time. Her muscles trembled with the effort not to move and she was grateful that Blake didn't hold it against her.

The only thing she wanted held against her was his hand, higher and harder.

Her fingers clenched and unclenched as the tension built. She knew what was going to happen—he'd reach the juncture of her thighs and then he'd stop to torture her some more. Kaia didn't know if she could stand it. In fact, she might have to light her own fuse.

Well, now, there was an idea. Why not? She had a couple of free hands and a couple of free nipples. She cupped her breasts and squeezed.

"Hey." Blake's hand stopped, but now Kaia didn't care.

She plucked at her nipples and rubbed against his thighs.

"You're breaking the no-moving rule."

Kaia threw back her head and moaned.

"But I like it," Blake said.

Kaia shivered. Her desire intensified, concentrating in a tiny knot of need. She moved faster, but it wasn't enough; she couldn't get the right angle because her legs were too far apart.

And then unexpectedly, blessedly, Blake's hand cupped her with just the right pressure in just the right spot.

For an instant, everything stopped. Time, sensation, sound. And then warm pleasure bloomed through her like petals unfurling. Kaia let the relief float through her. Nice. Blooming was nice. Not an explosion, but very, very nice.

"You've been a naughty girl," Blake murmured. "Spoiling your appetite like that."

"Hmm." Kaia stretched her arms over her head. The tension seeped out of her muscles leaving her limp and relaxed. "Well." She patted the side of his leg. "I guess I'll be going now."

Pretending to stand, she collapsed in laughter when Blake grabbed her hips and kept her firmly in place. "You guessed wrong."

She gestured to his lap. "But you're not dressed for the party."

Keeping one hand on her hip, Blake tore open the condom packet with his teeth.

Once more, Kaia reached for his zipper and once more Blake stopped her. "Your zipper privileges have been suspended. Don't move and keep your hands where I can see them."

She snorted and then clamped her hands over her mouth to stifle the laughter.

"Again, not an attractive sound. You're lucky the rest of you makes up for it."

"And you're lucky that I *will* make up for it," she said when he was ready.

Kaia raised herself on her knees, leaned forward and kissed him, aware of his hands gripping her hips. But he didn't take control, didn't try to hurry things along even though he was clearly more than ready for her.

Kaia didn't mean to spend so long kissing him, enjoying the hot sweetness, and she certainly didn't expect to feel her own desire start building again.

She heard a moan—it could have been his or it could have been hers. Grabbing the gate with one hand, she supported herself on his shoulder with the other and slowly lowered, taking him in inch by inch, wanting to make him wait the way he'd made her wait.

His hands spasmed on her hips and with a guttural, "Kaia!" he moved her up and down, setting an increasingly faster, harder pace.

And she was right there with him, feeling the pressure building again until, with a final, deep thrust, Blake groaned her name and shuddered. She rocked once more and felt a hot rush of exploding sensation.

Gulping for air, she collapsed against his sweaty torso, her own skin also slick. Her hand hurt where she'd gripped the metal lattice.

Her heart hurt because she knew she would never find a connection like this with anyone else.

"Kaia?" Blake stroked her back.

Lovely, but it was so very warm. She pulled back and fanned her face. "Okay. Long fuse, big explosion. Got it."

Blake captured one of her hands and pressed a kiss to her palm, as he'd done before. "This was about more than a big explosion."

Kaia stilled, unsure whether she wanted him to continue or not. Once he said whatever he was going to say, it couldn't be unsaid. "Or, in my case, a couple of explosions."

He shook his head. "I'm serious."

Kaia's heart had just started to slow down and now it kicked back up again. "Blake," she began. She didn't know what she was going to say, but she wanted to give him time to think and get past the immediate post-sex glow before he made promises he'd regret.

"Kaia, I can't erase—"

"Folks," Luke's voice interrupted. "I've been informed that the entire East Coast is blacked out due to a power grid failure. We're going to be here for a while."

11

A BLACKOUT.

Alarmed chatter drowned out Luke's next few sentences. Blake cocked his head, straining to hear, hoping Luke's announcement hadn't caused hysteria. All it took was one person to lose it and the crowd would feed on the panic. The next few seconds were crucial. Luke would have to maintain control. And he shouldn't have to do it by himself.

Blake punched the gate in frustration, which accomplished nothing except making his knuckles hurt.

"The whole East Coast?" Kaia repeated.

His attention swung back to her. He'd been about to tell her that he couldn't erase the past and ask for her to give them another chance. He still needed to say it, and more, but he'd have to wait until later.

"Yes." He brushed a few stray hairs from her damp cheek and leaned forward to kiss her, but she was already shifting off his legs.

"That means it'll be hours before the power comes back on."

They stared at each other. If ever there was a cue

for one of them to give a cheesy smile and say, "However will we pass the time?" this was it. But he could only think that it also meant hours with all those people downstairs and Blake caught behind the gate. Hours with his professional reputation on the line and nothing he could do about it. He couldn't even communicate with Luke. He felt like punching the gate again when he should be holding Kaia and savoring what they'd just shared. She'd always liked the cuddling part, he remembered.

He reached for her to try and make up for his abrupt mood change, but heard rustling as Kaia rearranged her dress. "Kaia, come he—"

"You said Luke was your best guy?" she interrupted. Her back was to him as she stuck her leg through whatever underwear thing she was wearing.

"Yeah." He hesitated, feeling like a jerk. Grabbing his shirt, he drew it over his head and jammed his arms through the cuffs. "But I'm sure he's still wondering where the hell I am." Luke would notice that Kaia was also missing and make assumptions. He knew of their past. No way would he send somebody looking for them.

"You told him he was in charge."

Blake remembered. "But the circumstances have changed." Understatement. "I'm looking really bad, here."

"Honestly, I think you look pretty good." Kaia got lightly to her feet.

"You know what I mean."

"I do." Kaia leaned against the wall, watching as he finished dressing.

She was fast. His eyes had adjusted to the dark

enough for him to marvel at how cool and serene she looked when minutes earlier, she'd been anything but.

"What would you be doing if you were downstairs?" she asked.

Blake got to his feet. "Working on getting us out of here."

"By doing what?"

"I don't know—trying to start the generator. Something." Truthfully, there wasn't much he could do, since that was the way he'd designed the system.

"If there's a generator, why isn't it running?"

"It's programmed to require manual activation if the security system deploys."

"I know you've got men stationed outside," Kaia said. "Why haven't they started it?"

Blake exhaled as he strapped on his holster. "It needs a code, too."

"Wow," she said. "You put a lot of thought into this."

That made him feel kind of good. He gave a last shake to the gate and admired the installation. "I guess that's the bright spot. At least I know I've designed a foolproof system."

A couple of beats went by. "There are always ways around a system."

And she'd taught him those methods. "Not this system. No one can get in or out until we want them getting in or out."

Kaia laughed. "I can."

Her words hung in the silence between them.

Did she think he'd forgotten all the little tricks and techniques she'd revealed to him? "Well, sure, if you blow holes in the walls."

"Oh, please." She grimaced. "I've got more finesse than that."

Now she'd piqued his curiosity. "You, ah, took a look around?"

She lifted a shoulder. "A little."

"And you seriously think you can get out?"

"And back in."

In the background, Blake heard a shrill voice going on about medicine and Luke's calm reply. He couldn't make out the words, because Luke wasn't trying to be heard above the crowd, but he knew the drill. Luke would be reassuring the woman that they were doing everything they could and so on and so on.

From here on out, the situation would only deteriorate. "Okay." Blake knew Kaia wasn't going to offer; he was going to have to ask. "Show me. Please," he tacked on.

Without a word, Kaia took off down the hall toward the bedrooms, leaving Blake to trot after her. He'd turned on his flashlight, but she didn't appear to need one.

She led him to the sauna in the home gym. "This is one of two possibilities. It depends on whether you want to re-enter the house or not."

Blake was disappointed. He pointed to the interior window facing outside the house. "That's not ordinary glass."

"I know." She walked inside the sauna and gestured for him to join her. "I'd use weights to smash it—but only if I were in a hurry and didn't care if anyone heard."

"And then what?" He looked out into the blackness. "That's a sheer drop to concrete."

"I didn't say getting out would be easy. I'd either go up and find a better place to climb down, or I'd rappel down."

Right. He waved his flashlight at her. "And you just so happen to have rappelling equipment on you."

She simply looked at him.

I've got a lot in my pockets... A whole bunch of ugly emotions started swirling within him: distrust, betrayal, wariness, and doubt. Blake exhaled heavily and blew them away. This time, he was going with his basic gut feelings. "Okay, I'm a Boy Scout. You're a Girl Scout. What's the second way?"

"The bathroom." She started walking toward it.

"What? The little window?" He'd measured it and the one just like it in the hall bath. "Nobody can get through that window."

"You'd be surprised."

Blake had a feeling he would be.

"Besides, I could put jewelry in a canister and shoot it outside and pick it up later."

He followed her into the master bathroom. "But you'd still be caught inside. And then we'd know to search and locate the canister."

"Not if I had an accomplice waiting."

Blake could visualize just such a scenario. He got the queasy bad-burrito-on-a-stakeout feeling in his stomach. "But you'd still be caught."

"I know." She pushed a vanity bench beneath the window. "That's why it's obviously not my first choice." Kaia hitched up her skirt and climbed onto the bench.

Blake momentarily flashed to her hitching up her skirt and climbing onto *him*. Incredible. He could hardly believe it had happened or that he was ready for it to happen again.

He looked up at her and knew he was ready for a lot to happen again. Whether Kaia could get out of here or not, he was going to convince her to give them a second chance together.

No, a first chance. Wipe the slate clean and start with who they were now. No pretending. No lying. The past would always be a part of their history, but it wouldn't define them.

Kaia was standing on her toes as she shined a concentrated beam around the windowsill. Her mini flashlight was better than his. He'd have to ask her where she got it.

"The window has been painted shut," she announced as she dug into one of her voluminous pockets—the ones that made him nervous. She withdrew something, he heard a snick, and guessed she'd unfolded a pocketknife which she was now running around the edge of the window.

She was very quiet and very efficient. Blake had never seen her in action before. He knew what she'd been and had listened when she'd told him snippets from her life, but he'd never actually visualized the details.

He felt a puff of welcome breeze and saw that she'd opened the window without him hearing. He should pay attention.

She pushed the window outward to the nine and three quarters of an inch clearance he'd previously measured.

"As I said, nobody is getting through there. And I'd go so far as to challenge you to get the right angle to shoot a canister anywhere but straight down," he said.

"You'd challenge me, would you?" Kaia was bent over, doing something.

Blake shined his flashlight at her in time to see her straighten. He heard a "psst" and a scraping sound. "Compressed air?"

"No."

She didn't elaborate. That was okay. He'd find out later.

After a wrenching creak, the entire window was in Kaia's hands. "Hold this for me, will you?"

Stunned, Blake automatically took the glass from her and set it on the bathroom counter. When he turned back, Kaia was leaning halfway out the opening.

"What is that—eighteen…twenty inches? You still can't get through that."

She didn't say anything.

"I've got quite a view here."

She wiggled her rump and he laughed and lightly smacked it. He couldn't resist.

"Hey, I am not into that," he heard.

"Just checking. Are you stuck?"

She popped back down. "I've been through smaller. I was just figuring out which way I was going after I got out."

As Kaia spoke, she tugged up the top of her dress, poking her arms through holes he hadn't known were there, covering her shoulders and chest and skimming fabric down her arms. The material had unfolded like an accordion.

Next, she pulled off the silver and black belt and tested its strength.

The queasy, bad burrito feeling returned.

"Calm down," she said. "Remember that I was hired to get Royce's cuffs back."

"How did you know what I was thinking?" he asked, rather than deny it.

"Your breathing changed and you cracked your knuckle."

He immediately unclenched his fist.

She straightened and pulled some more, tucked some more, and even though Blake shone his light on her, he couldn't figure out how the evening dress she'd been wearing had turned into a long-sleeved shirt, tights and a backpack.

"How…how did you do that?"

"Practice." She glanced up at him and kicked off her shoes. Ripping out the lining, she ended up wearing what appeared to be ballet flats. "Better for climbing," she explained. The shoes disappeared into the backpack.

Only her hands and face were exposed. The rest of her was covered in form-fitting black. She looked like, well, a cat burglar. And she'd transformed into one with a breathtaking efficiency he wasn't going to think about.

"I'm impressed," Blake admitted.

"Yeah, and you're worried, too." She exhaled heavily and looked him right in the eyes. "I guess you'll never completely trust me, will you?"

He hesitated. It wasn't intentional, but she noticed. "I—"

"Don't." She placed a finger over his lips, then kissed him, lightly and quickly.

It felt like a goodbye.

Stepping onto the vanity bench, she waggled her fingers. "See ya."

If Blake hadn't seen what happened next, he would never have believed it.

Kaia raised her leg and poked it through the window. Then she stretched her arms over her head an impossibly long way and her shoulders seemed to disappear. There were a couple of twists, a pop—did she dislocate her shoulder socket?—and she was straddling the ledge. Balancing herself, she maneuvered the backpack through the opening, shifted her hips and head and finally, Blake watched her remaining leg snake upward and she was gone.

He'd watched her and he still didn't believe it. Blake stepped onto the little vanity bench and looked out.

"Boo," Kaia said, her head hanging inches away.

"Kaia, my God, the drainpipe isn't meant to hold your weight!"

"It's not." She dropped and he barely heard the padded thud as she landed on the dormer to the left.

"Relax." Her whisper drifted up to him.

Blake's mouth was open so he must have gasped. He swallowed. "Don't fall," he managed to say.

"Don't plan to."

Blake glanced around the roof and sky. At least it wasn't raining anymore. In fact, the moon was trying to peek out of the thinning clouds. But the tiles were still shiny and had to be slippery.

Kaia looped her makeshift rope and tossed it upward a couple of times before it caught on something.

Blake didn't like how dangerous and iffy it looked. "Hey," he called softly. "You don't have to prove anything more. I'm convinced you could get away."

"Don't worry. This is nothing." She looked upward a moment and added, "Well, maybe something. As far as difficulty, this is only a three or four out of ten. Maybe as much as a five because of the rain." She tested her weight against the rope and when it held, she started climbing. "At least I don't have to jump across open spaces or walk a tightrope. I really hate that."

She was going to give him a heart attack with that kind of talk.

Just then, the moon poked through the clouds, and Blake got a clear view of Kaia easily climbing to the roof above them. At least she made it look easy, as only the most skilled can. Once on the ridge line, her figure in the tight outfit was silhouetted against the sky as she unhooked the rope.

She'd been so quick and so silent, in complete control of her body.

Blake knew that body. He'd recently been incredibly intimate with that body and yet he'd had no idea what it was capable of.

He watched, fascinated, as Kaia make her way across the rooftop, her movements gracefully sinuous. It was the hottest thing he'd ever seen and desire flared within him. He didn't even try to tamp it down. He would never forget the sight of Kaia in the moonlight, scampering over the gleaming tiles, as silent as a shadow until she disappeared over the other side and out of sight.

Wow. Blake stared after her, still admiring the way she'd efficiently gone through an opening he'd dismissed as not worth putting sensors on.

He wasn't going to make that mistake again.

Blake mentally redesigned some of his clients' installations as he breathed in the humid night air and enjoyed the breeze. He'd have to ask Kaia for hints about the transportation side of his business, too. For pay, of course. She deserved it. She could make big bucks as a security consultant. Maybe he should hire her permanently. He tested the idea, liking it more and more. Seeing her every day would reinforce their personal relationship.

Blake closed his eyes, the breeze on his face, and recalled the utter surprise of making love to Kaia with the possibility of discovery. He could get addicted to the extra punch that brought to sex. Kaia...

Had not come back. The desire that had flamed to life again went out. Blake opened his eyes, waiting for her head to pop back into sight. He replayed their conversation and couldn't recall Kaia telling him where she was going. Well, obviously she was going to try and get back into the house. But then what? They hadn't discussed a plan because Blake hadn't believed she could really escape. But she had.

He stared at the spot where she'd disappeared over the top of the roof, straining to hear. Would she find Luke and tell him what had happened? Blake should have given her a message…but if Luke saw her in that getup, would he listen to her?

And what exactly would she say?

Then again, why assume she'd seek out Luke?

Or Royce, for that matter. Suppose she was planning to keep the cuffs? Or maybe she made the whole story up and he'd just been conned by a thief.

Blake slowly stepped off the bench and sat on it, slumping against the wall.

Had he just made an incredibly stupid, stupid mistake?

What reason did Kaia have to return for him? Did he honestly think he was such a hot lover that it would make up for sending her to prison?

I guess you'll never completely trust me, will you?

And the quick goodbye kiss. He felt sick—worse than any food poisoning. He wanted to trust her. He wanted to make up for not believing her before, but did that mean he should believe her now?

It was a lot harder to break in than it was to break out. From the other side of the roof, Kaia took a moment to gaze at the darkened landscape. Car headlights bounced slowly along the road and she could see pinpoints of light through windows or from someone walking outside with a flashlight. The night was quiet without the hum from the air conditioning units. She did hear the motor from a van in the drive below. It was unmarked, so it must belong to Blake's crew. The crumpled valet awning blocked the front pathway to the house and she didn't see anyone standing around.

Turning back to the window, Kaia removed it from the frame and carefully lowered it as far as she could inside before letting go. There was a thud and a rattle, but since she'd removed the wooden sill with it, the glass apparently survived. This window was easier to get in and out of since the architect had thoughtfully provided a handy decorative protrusion to stand on.

Seconds later, Kaia was inside the hall bathroom. Fortunately, it was vacant. She opened the door to the hallway and made a dramatic, "Ta da!" type entrance, but Blake wasn't waiting by the gate.

Maybe he hadn't expected her to be so quick. She waited for a couple of minutes before walking in the opposite direction to the open part of the hall that overlooked the party room.

Now that she was back inside, she noticed how warm it was getting in the house. She peeked over the landing's banister to the room below and saw people sitting in chairs, surrounded by candlelight, chatting away, while others had staked out the couches and looked to be sleeping. A few of the younger crowd were on the floor. She didn't see Royce, but she couldn't see the band or the bar area from this angle.

No one was looking up, but Kaia didn't want to attract attention. Keeping to the shadows, she moved down the hallway toward the stairs until she could see the far end of the room where Casper's office was located.

Life would be so much easier if she could just nip downstairs, get into the office, and unload the snuff-box. Then she wouldn't have to worry about Blake or anyone else discovering that she had it.

As she watched, trying to decide whether she should risk it or not, a stealthy movement caught her attention. If anyone knew stealth, it was Kaia.

People trying not to attract attention by sneaking around were more noticeable than if they moved as though they had a right to be where they were.

If anyone had a right to be wherever she wanted in this house, it was Tina Nazario, and that's who was sneaking over to her husband's office door.

She was carrying a candle, which she set on one of the jewelry display pedestals. Kaia hoped wax didn't drip on the velvet—kind of a strange thought to be having at this moment, but there it was.

Tina glanced over her shoulder to see if she was being watched, and Kaia shook her head. What an amateur move. And judging by the stash upstairs, Tina was no amateur.

She bent over the doorknob.

She's picking the lock. How interesting.

Tina took long enough to get inside for Kaia to know that while she wasn't an expert, she'd certainly picked a lock or two in her time.

"Kaia!" Blake was at the gate.

Drawing her finger to her lips in the universal sign to be quiet, she gestured for him to wait. They didn't have to wait long. Half-a-minute later, Tina quickly slipped out of the office and closed the door behind her.

That could not be good, Kaia thought as she ran lightly toward Blake. "Where have you been?"

"You're okay," he said on an exhale. Even in the dim light, she could see that his face was pale.

She blinked. "Were you *worried* about me?"

He extended a finger through the grating and brushed her cheek. "I thought…" He cleared his throat. "When you didn't come back…"

"You thought I'd fall down and go boom?"

He gave a surprised laugh. "Well, yeah."

"The idea was to show you I could get around your system, Blake. That means getting out *and* getting back in." She gestured to the gate. "You will note that we are now on opposite sides of the gate."

"I'm…"

"Clearly stunned. I'm not sure if that's a compliment or an insult."

His mouth twisted in a rueful grimace. "If it had given you more trouble, it would be better for my ego."

"I'm just really, really good. Does that help?"

"Not so much. Hey." He leaned forward against the gate. "I don't want anything to be between us ever again."

She leaned forward, too. "So whatcha gonna do about it?"

"I'll think of something." He bent down and she stood on tiptoe and they kissed through the grating.

Kaia raised her hand and met his there. They linked fingers and pressed against each other, mouths clinging through the gate.

They probably looked ridiculous, but Kaia didn't care. As soon as he saw that she was on the other side, he could have started barking orders at her, giving her instructions about what he wanted her to do. Instead, he was kissing her, letting her know that she was more important than his responsibilities or his reputation, or anything else.

She melted into the kiss a little more and felt the weight of the snuffbox at her waist both literally and figuratively. Once she was out from under that, once she'd completed her job for Casper, then the future was a blank slate and there *would* be nothing between them.

She squeezed Blake's fingers and they broke apart. "You're amazing," he said.

She smiled. "So far."

"Have you talked to Luke?"

"I haven't been downstairs. But I did see Tina skulking around. She went into Casper's office."

"Kaia, she lives here. She can go anywhere she wants."

"So why is she sneaking around and picking locks?"

Kaia could tell by Blake's expression that she didn't need to spell it out.

"This could become incredibly awkward." He stared past her toward the stairs. "I need you to tell Luke to keep an eye on her and where I am. And I'll need an earpiece."

"You can tell him yourself."

Blake reared back. "I thought we were together in this."

"Jeez, Blake! You can tell him yourself, because I'm going to come and get you."

"Nooo." He shook his head. "No way can I get through that window."

Kaia grinned at him. "Trust me."

12

"YOU'RE ENJOYING this, aren't you?" Blake held Kaia's hands in a death grip.

"Little bit." Facing him, she backed her way up the roof.

Yeah. She was climbing backward.

The curved clay tiles were slippery, especially for Blake who was wearing regular shoes. Kaia had tried to convince him to try the climb barefoot, but he felt he'd be good to go with the rubber soles. That might have been a mistake.

Then again, he'd never believed he'd actually get through the window. But by Kaia removing the wooden frame and showing him how to position his body—and a whole lot of pushing and tugging on her part—Blake had worked his shoulders through the opening. After that, it was a piece of cake to get the rest of him through.

They'd had to cannibalize some of the gym equipment for wire to rig extra support for Blake's weight—and he'd really objected to that—but here they were, on the roof, climbing toward the ridge line on their way to the other bathroom window.

Kaia backed up and Blake inched toward her, his foot slipping before it found a good hold. He grabbed her hands even tighter.

"I've got you. Trust me." She was so calm and seemingly unconcerned.

"Trust isn't the issue. Me out-weighing you by a hundred pounds is the issue."

"It's all about leverage."

Blake slipped a bit again. "I should have listened to you and taken off my shoes."

"Maybe not. I didn't realize you had rubber soles."

"That's in case we have to chase somebody." He looked over his shoulder. "I don't think it helps for climbing on wet tile."

"Don't look down," she instructed.

"I don't have a problem with heights." Yet he wasn't exactly *enjoying* looking down.

"I've heard that before."

As they approached the ridge line, Blake could see what was on the other side and he wasn't looking forward to it. At least on this side of the house they had grass to break their fall. On the front, there was only the driveway.

"Don't think about it." She was reading his mind.

"Then give me something else to think about."

"Okay. Answer a question for me." She pointed to where she wanted him to place his foot. "Why did you have to go undercover?"

Blake stopped staring at his feet and met her eyes. "That came out of nowhere."

"I've been wondering. You knew I had the Cat's Eye diamond. I never hid it. Why go the fake boyfriend route? And for so long? Weeks. You let me…" She swallowed. *"Why?"*

The clouds had mostly cleared and a partial moon gleamed down. Kaia's face showed more emotion than he'd ever seen. Hurt and betrayal and a tortured bewilderment.

He hated that he was responsible for those emotions and he hated that if it was part of his job, he'd probably do it again. Thank God it wasn't his job anymore.

Blake knew his answer would anger her and this wasn't the time for Kaia to get emotional. He chose his words carefully. "We wanted to know if you'd acted alone."

A few seconds went by before she understood. "My parents." She gazed off to the side. "You were using me to get to my parents and uncle."

"And anyone in their circle."

"You didn't." She looked back at him. "How disappointing for you."

"I got chewed out, yeah."

She made a face. "So did I." She started backing up again.

That was it? No explosion? "Is there going to be yelling now?" Blake asked, very aware that they were on a rooftop and his footing was none too secure.

"From me? No. I asked. You answered. Now I know." Her face had gone blank again.

That was too easy. He should explain more. "I dragged it out so I could be with you longer. I should have pressured you harder to meet your family. But I didn't. I told myself you'd get suspicious. But it was just an excuse to stay with you."

"Now *that* makes me mad."

Great. "I thought it would make you feel better!"

"Hmm." She gazed off as though considering.

"Prolonging a lie for your own selfish reasons… No. I don't feel better."

Neither did Blake. "Why don't you just shove me off the roof now then and get it over with?"

"I'm rehabilitating you. Hold on there." She pointed to a reinforced opening around a vent. "I want to check for loose tiles."

She left him clinging to the side of the roof as she checked the ridge line. "I did bring up you meeting my parents. They told me you were a cop and I told them you'd already told me. They said I couldn't trust you and it came down to choosing either them or you. I chose you and moved in." She looked off into the distance. "I wonder whatever happened to that last bag of dirty laundry?"

Blake hadn't realized she'd moved in. He'd just thought she was sleeping over. A lot. Was he going to tell her that? Hell, no. "I didn't realize I'd come between you and your parents. I'm sorry." And he was, but not for the way she probably assumed. If they'd managed to arrest the whole bunch, Kaia might not have served any time at all.

"Don't be. At least not for that." She momentarily disappeared over the ridge line and her voice drifted back to him. "Things hadn't been that great between us since I figured out what they did."

"But…how could you not have known?"

She reappeared and gestured for him to climb toward her. "Keep to your left. There are some wonky areas."

He started climbing while she watched. "When I was little, it was mostly games and party tricks. A portion of my parents' business was making copies of jewelry pieces for insurance purposes."

For when clients didn't want to risk wearing the real thing, Blake knew.

"Part of my dad's sales pitch to have a duplicate made was proving how vulnerable a client's safe was. He'd take me along on his calls and nobody paid attention to me, a little kid. I'd do my thing, and then my dad would parade me and whatever I'd recovered, and get the commission. 'Look at that. Your safe is so flimsy, a child can break into it.'"

Blake glanced up to where she crouched, waiting for him. "You heard that a lot."

"Oh, yeah. The day he couldn't ignore the fact that I had breasts was the saddest day in his life."

"I promise never to ignore your breasts," Blake told her.

She made a strange sound and gestured with her foot. "Pay attention to your climbing."

He grinned and looked down again. "So what was their scam—giving clients back two copies?"

"Probably. Or returning the original missing some stones. But I didn't know that. And when I got older and asked more questions, my parents always had an answer that made sense."

Blake reached the ridge line and sat, straddling it. Kaia started to move, but he stopped her. "Wait. Tell me the rest. When did you figure it out?"

She sat next to him. "They sent me to a ritzy boarding school so they'd have an in with the other parents. Up till then, I'd been home-schooled. I was just so happy to finally get to go some place and be around people my own age. To have friends." She turned away. "I don't like talking about it."

"I don't like your parents a whole lot." Blake swung

his other leg over the top of the roof. "They manipulated you. You were just a kid."

"Not all the time." She stood and looked down at him. "I got invited to go on a ski trip with a friend and her family. First time, ever. Only time, ever. They robbed the house while we were gone. I know they did. They never admitted it, but when we got back, her parents discovered the break-in. I recognized the technique. Dad was getting old and clumsy."

Some day, Blake hoped he'd meet her parents so he could tell them exactly what he thought of them. "Kaia, that wasn't your fault."

She handed him the end of a rope she'd tied around her waist. "I knew they'd try something. I shouldn't have gone. And afterward, when I wouldn't accept any other invitations, they yanked me out of the school. Speaking of yanking—try not to. Use the rope to keep your balance."

"Forget it." He tossed the rope back at her. "If I slip I'd take you with me."

"Then don't slip."

"Kaia—"

"Blake." She put the rope in his hand. "I'd slow you enough to give you a chance to get your footing."

He decided to quit arguing, but he had no intention of using the rope.

Blake stood and surveyed the scene below. It was strangely dark with little pockets of light here and there. In the distance, streets full of vehicles were either gridlocked or moved sluggishly without the traffic signals.

"Follow me," Kaia said. "Put your feet exactly where I put mine."

"Wait." When she turned back he found it surprisingly hard to ask his question. "Did you do any jobs after that—after the ski trip?"

They stared at each other. "What do you think?" she snapped, and took off across the roof top.

Blake struggled to keep up. "I think you were forced into it."

Without warning, she stopped and whirled around. If he'd tried a move like that, he would have ended up on the ground.

"Don't make excuses for me. Don't make me into something I'm not. Something more palatable to your sense of right and wrong. I didn't have much of a choice, but I had one. I could have turned my parents into the police, gone to a foster home until I was eighteen. But I didn't."

"Who would have? Kaia, they're your parents!"

"So? We can't afford family loyalty. I haven't seen or spoken to them since I called them after I was arrested. I wouldn't know how to get in touch with them even if I wanted to. So don't get any ideas."

Blake was horrified. He couldn't begin to comprehend a family dynamic like the one Kaia had. "That's not why I asked."

"It doesn't matter. The point is that I knew what I was doing. I agreed to go on jobs if they'd give me college money. But once I enrolled, I was done with them. That's why I thought Casper's job was a godsend. It bought me another year. But Blake, don't pretty it up in your mind. For two years, I knew exactly what I was doing." She drew a breath. "I wasn't guilty of the crime I went to prison for, but I was guilty of others. I've paid. Now, I can move on."

She met his gaze defiantly, clearly expecting him to be repulsed when he felt exactly the opposite.

"You think that's going to scare me away?" he asked.
"Does it?"

"No."

"Because you feel sorry for me?"

"Because you're taking responsibility for your actions." Her integrity pinged his buttons more than anything else right now. Blake wasn't falling off the roof, he was falling in love. Had fallen in love. "That's hot."

Her eyes narrowed. "Are you joking? I just told you that I'm no Girl Scout—"

"And I don't care. I mean, I *care,* but it's not a deal breaker." The conversation was too intense to be held in such a dangerous place.

"A…deal breaker?" Kaia was looking at him as though he'd grown two heads. "Do we have a deal?"

"Yes." He took a step, wobbled and regained his balance. "Our deal is you get me off this roof and I'll let you have your wicked way with me."

"I've already had my wicked way with you."

"You've only got one way?"

A surprised burst of laughter escaped from her. "I have many ways."

"Good. You can pick. Deal?"

"What if I say no?"

"Then, I'll pick."

"I meant, what if I leave you on the roof?"

"You won't." Blake placed the end of the rope into her palm and closed her fingers over it. "I trust you."

Kaia looked at her hand. "What's that supposed to be…some kind of symbolism?"

"Well…yeah." And he thought it was pretty good, too.

"Being stupid equals trust?"

"No." She was so prickly. "I just…wanted you to

know that I…trust you." He opened his arms. "I accept you for who you are. All of you."

"Blake." She gave him back the rope. "I appreciate that you're feeling all touchy feely because of my 'poor little me' story, but just hang on to the rope, okay?"

So much for grand gestures. "Okay."

When he thought about it, as he followed Kaia across steep angles of slippery tile, he figured she was the one trusting him to let go and not drag her down if he found himself heading for the ground. He watched where she put her feet, didn't argue when she pointed to handholds and accepted that she was the expert and he was a big guy on a slippery slope. It was a different experience for Blake not to be the authority in a situation, but no less adrenaline-charged. He figured this was one of those character-building situations. That didn't mean he liked it. Still, he tried not to let his ego get in the way, even though he caught Kaia taking a safer, but longer route.

"We could go over that way." He pointed to the decorative part of the house's elevation. "I'm a pretty good jumper."

"You'd slide into the drainage valley and probably crash through to the attic."

"I—"

"Blake." She gave him a don't-argue-with-me look. He surrendered. "Fine."

"There're plenty of places you can show off when we get to the front of the house."

"I said 'fine.'"

She could have left him with *some* ego. That's when he saw the three dormers and knew right away that he was going to end up trusting his life to a decorative flourish the builders probably slapped together in fifteen minutes.

"We're going for the middle one."

"Those look like dollhouse roofs." And they didn't look as though they'd support him, let alone both of them. His heartbeat kicked up a notch.

Kaia held onto the edge of the roof and let herself down until she stood on the dormer, her head about two feet below where Blake perched.

"I've already removed the sill, so there should be enough room for you to get in. Watch me. When you do it, I'll be right here and can guide you inside. Tie your end of the rope through your belt loops."

Blake did not like this.

She disappeared inside. What was there to watch? One instant she was standing there and the next, she was gone. Blake studied the drop and the miniature roof. Where, exactly, was he supposed to put his feet?

He looked down at the concrete pebbled drive below.

"Don't look down," he heard.

"How do you know I'm looking down?"

She stuck her head out. "'Cause you're not in front of the window."

If he dropped and his feet slipped, he'd be straddling the thing like a horse. Ouch.

"Hey. You can do it. Trust me." Her smile showed all her teeth.

"Sure I can do it," he said. "Though maybe not successfully."

He studied the drop, below the drop, and Kaia's head for several moments.

"Hey," she said again.

"What?"

Her head disappeared and a naked leg replaced it. "We had a deal. It's wicked way time."

Well, when she put it like that…Blake eased over the

edge of the roof, grateful for all the pull-ups he'd done in the gym, and lowered himself carefully to the little dormer. Squatting, he peered underneath through the window.

Barelegged, illuminated by a flashlight propped next to the mirror, Kaia sat on the bathroom counter and crooked her finger.

All righty then.

Odd how Blake was no longer concerned with the drop or the hard driveway below. His feet naturally found a hold and he miraculously remembered the way Kaia had shown him how to position his body to get through the window. He didn't even need her to hop off the counter and help him. He was motivated. Highly motivated.

"You're going to hurt yourself," she cautioned as he forced his shoulders through the opening.

"Nah. It's okay." What was a little pain compared to the pleasure waiting on the counter?

He paused halfway through, but Kaia spread her legs apart a few inches. Blake was socked with a combination of dizziness and lust and the next thing he knew, he was dropping head first through the window of the Nazarios' guest bathroom.

Rolling, he got to his feet. "That," he said, "is an excellent look for you."

She leaned back against the mirror and gave him a half-smile.

The danger was over but the adrenaline still coursed through Blake's body. One more crook of Kaia's finger and he was standing between her legs, his mouth fused to hers.

"I can't believe we did that," he murmured. "You, alone, over the roof was incredible, but to take me with you was miraculous." He kissed her again. "I can't believe it." He was repeating himself.

"You're talking too much," she whispered and reached for his zipper. This time, he let her clever fingers inside to stroke his hard length. His muscles quivered. Everything quivered. His brain shut down.

"You really liked that," she said.

"I really like you."

"I can tell."

She had no idea. Blake kissed her as though his life depended on it because he suspected that it did. He didn't care about anything else but Kaia at this moment. He wanted her as he'd never wanted anything in his life.

He wanted her *in* his life. He wanted her smiling and making him feel as though the world was perfect. And he was going to do anything it took to put that smile on her face.

Caressing her hair and holding her cheeks, he used his kisses to tell her how he felt without words.

When she wrapped her legs around his waist, he thrust into her, clutching her to his chest as he stared at their reflection in the mirror behind her. He barely recognized himself or the rapt expression that would have concerned him had he been with anyone else but Kaia.

She threw back her head and moaned, clamping her lips together to swallow the sound. The combination of danger, adrenaline, the erotic shadows, and Kaia, herself, brought him to an almost instant climax, one he was helpless to hold back. He thrust deeply and exploded, the force causing him to see bright colors kalaidescoping behind his eyelids. He couldn't move. He couldn't think and was barely aware of Kaia rocking hard against him as she gripped his shoulders.

He gulped air as he heard her low moans, glad she'd been with him because he was completely spent. They clung together, shaking, or maybe Blake was the one who was shaking. It didn't matter. He opened his eyes to meet his reflection and silently vowed that nothing and no one would ever hurt the woman in his arms again.

"Danger makes a great aphrodisiac," she whispered.

"Yeah," he agreed eloquently. And then, "I love you."

He felt her go quiet before she looked up at him. "That's the adrenaline talking."

"Doesn't mean it isn't true."

She studied him silently.

Blake understood and didn't blame her. "You don't have to say it back," he told her. "It won't change how I feel."

"Tell me again when this is all over. Tell me when you're back to your life and I'm back to mine. Tell me when you've had a chance to think."

He didn't need to think. He knew. Blake kissed the top of her head. "Deal."

13

"READY?"

Kaia, her dress back to looking like a dress, nodded. She and Blake had their plan and were going to part ways at the bottom of the stairs. Kaia would find Royce and Blake would track down Luke and see if anyone had noticed Tina's activities.

Kaia descended first, keeping to the shadows as much as possible. Seconds later, Blake did the same.

When Blake had told her he loved her, she'd almost, *almost* told him about the snuffbox. For him to really mean it, and for her to believe he loved her, he needed to know everything.

But something had held her back. They needed cooler heads—cooler bodies. A cooler time.

Kaia glided toward Royce, who was sitting in the conversation pit at the end of the room near Casper's office. The table was covered with candles and Royce held a penlight over some papers as a gray-haired man signed them. The woman next to him—Kaia presumed it was his wife—was admiring a chunky ring on her hand.

Kaia stayed in the shadows until the couple left, and then approached Royce as he put away the paperwork.

"Hey," she said softly. "Got turquoise?"

His head snapped up and his eyes brightened. "Did you…?"

Nodding, Kaia bent down and placed the cuffs on the table in front of him.

Royce stared at them, his lips pressed tightly together. Kaia was a little surprised at the emotion she saw him holding back. She'd known they were important to him, but she hadn't *known*. It made her feel as though she'd done something good for once and she liked it. She should be thanking *him*.

He cleared his throat. "If there is ever—"

"Do you know where my parents are?" she asked suddenly.

Royce looked up, startled, and then leaned back. "No." He eyed her carefully.

"But you could find them."

He hesitated and then shrugged. "I could possibly get a message to them. Do you have such a message?"

"Other than go to hell? No."

"Kaia." Royce gave her a long look as though he was disappointed in her.

Was he serious? "They let me go to prison. I couldn't even afford a lawyer!"

"Refresh my memory…how much of your sentence did you serve?"

What did that have to do with it? "Less than a fourth."

"And why was that?"

"Because the government needed me to do them a favor."

"Oh, right." He nodded. "And how is it that out of all

the specialized government personnel and all the talent in all the prisons that *you* were chosen?"

Was Royce implying that her parents had had something to do with it?

"And, how convenient that Wendell Yost of Guardian was not only willing to sponsor your parole, but to provide you with a top-notch lawyer?"

Kaia assumed it was because she was making a lot of money for Wendell.

Royce tapped a finger against his mouth. "And correct me if I'm wrong, but you continue to have these little jobs come your way, do you not?"

"Yes," Kaia said, slowly.

"You were also quite lucky to find a furnished apartment. Overseas owners wanted to have it occupied… an extremely reasonable rent if you signed a two-year lease… It just seemed to fall into place for you."

"Ty-Tyrone found it."

"Who found it for Tyrone?"

"Did you?" she asked, already knowing the answer.

Royce shook his head.

Her parents. Kaia blinked. "I thought—"

"As you were meant to."

So her parents hadn't totally abandoned her. It would take time for Kaia to get past the years of hating them. And it was unlikely they'd ever have a family reunion, complete with picnic and potato salad, but it helped to know they weren't totally devoid of feelings.

"So do you have a message for them?" Royce asked.

"Tell them I'm okay."

"They know you're okay."

She gazed across the room to where she saw Blake talking to Luke. "Tell them I'm…happy." She smiled. "Very happy." And realized it was the truth.

Royce cleared his throat. "There is another matter."

"*Another* matter? You sure have a lot of matters."

Royce reached into his pocket. "I found this." He slid a mangled earpiece across the table.

"Blake's. The dog ran off with it," she told him.

"Yeah, well, I didn't know whether to give it to the big guy or not," Royce said.

"Where is Jo Jo?"

"Tina put her in a room off the kitchen. But the dog isn't our problem. Our hostess's sticky fingers are the problem."

Kaia exhaled. "What's missing?"

"A Tahitian pearl earring."

"Just one?"

"The other was in someone's ear."

"Oh."

"I saw her take it, but I don't know if she's still got it. She's been going in and out of here." Royce indicated the office.

"I saw her once, myself," Kaia said. She watched Blake for a couple of moments. He was involved with Luke and some other men. Now was the time to unload the snuffbox. "I'm going to take a look."

"Want me to run interference?" Royce asked.

"Light interference. Don't blow your cover."

"I'm not undercover!"

"Blake's already suspicious because of me."

"I'm the injured party here," she heard Royce grumble as she melted into the shadows and approached the office door. It was unlocked, thanks to Tina, and Kaia slipped inside. She actually felt a few internal butterflies as she clicked on her flashlight and realized how close she was to her goal. Before anything else, Kaia crossed to the vase where she was supposed to leave the snuffbox and felt inside. To her surprise, her fingers closed over a familiar lump and she withdrew the Cat's Eye pendant.

For a moment, she held it in the beam of light and admired the glitter.

It was hers. Twice she'd earned it, but it wasn't as valuable as what else Casper had promised. Carefully, Kaia put the snuffbox in the vase and then slipped the pendant back, as well.

If Casper was setting a trap, she wasn't taking the bait. She was going to make him hand her the pendant, preferably with Tyrone looking on.

Now that she'd delivered the snuffbox, she could deal with Tina. When Kaia had seen her come in here, Tina hadn't spent much time, so it was unlikely she'd hidden anything in a safe. Kaia glanced around the room and then, with a shrug, tried the pencil drawer in Casper's desk. It slid open and Kaia actually gasped. Gleaming in the beam of her flashlight was the leopard—cheetah—bracelet that Tyrone's wife had admired.

No way. What was with Tina and bracelets? And earrings, too, apparently.

Kaia slipped the bracelet into her pocket and checked out the rest of the room. She found a watch in an empty ice bucket on the credenza, a pair of eyeglasses behind a book, and a pen in the plant by the shuttered French doors.

If the things had been on Casper's desk, Kaia wouldn't have thought anything of it, but hidden as they were, she knew Tina had taken them from her guests. Maybe not tonight's guests, but guests some time.

Collecting the objects, she left the office and headed straight for Blake. He smiled when he saw her, but she shook her head and gestured for him to join her away from the people.

"What's up?" Still smiling, his gaze moved over her face sending a little warming feeling through her.

"For starters, here." She gave him the chewed-on earpiece. "Royce found it."

Blake examined the plastic. "And he chose to give it to you. Interesting."

"Not as interesting as what I found in Casper's office." She showed him.

"Kaia," he began with fake pleasantness, "why did you take it upon yourself to search Casper's office?"

Kaia didn't have time for a turf war. "I work for Guardian Security."

Blake looked utterly taken aback, as though that was the last thing in the world he'd expected her to say.

"Okay," he said slowly. "But why are you here to-night?"

"The cuffs." Officially. "Casper didn't want anyone to know about Tina. Speaking of, a Tahitian pearl earring is still missing. Royce saw her take it."

"Oh, man." Blake looked over her shoulder. Kaia figured he was watching Tina.

"She's probably lifted other stuff we don't know about," he said.

"Probably."

"Luke says that officials estimate power will be back on line in the morning." He rubbed his jaw and exhaled. "When people gather their things to get ready to leave, it'll be a mess."

"Yes."

Blake looked at her.

"Yes," Kaia said.

"I didn't say anything."

"You were going to ask if I'd try to get the earring off Tina."

"I was thinking about it," he admitted.

"I'm on it. It's likely that she still has it on her."

"I appreciate it. And have Royce pack up, will you? We should start inventorying."

Kaia nodded. Blake looked tired. She touched his arm. "Don't worry. It'll all work out."

BLAKE WATCHED KAIA thread her way across the room. He was going to have a chat with Casper when this was all over. He didn't even have to bring up Kaia; the behavior of Tina was bad enough. He thought of the reports of theft that spotted the area and suspected it was Tina's doing. The sad thing was that she'd been great for Blake's business.

He figured he'd lose the Nazarios as clients over this, maybe all the clients they'd sent his way, but knowing what the man had done to Kaia, he wasn't sorry. Together, they could build the business again.

Kaia approached Tina, stopped, leaned forward and said something to her, lightly touched the woman's shoulder, and then moved away. Blake figured she was setting up her attempt. He wondered when she'd actually lift the earring when Kaia reached the other side of the room, turned, and held up her hand.

She already had it? No way. He'd been watching, had known she was going to make the attempt, and had still missed it. She was scary good. He blew her a kiss, glad she was on his side.

KAIA SHARED TINA-WATCHING duties with Blake for the rest of the night.

Around eight o'clock in the morning, there were a

series of clicks and the house hummed back to life. Light illuminated a roomful of sleepy guests who sat up and looked around. The players in an all-night poker game kept dealing.

Blake's office sent whatever codes or signals needed to be sent and suddenly, the shades retracted and in the distance, Kaia heard gates sliding back into the walls. Sunlight flooded the room and the real work began. As the rest of the crowd awoke and blinked against the sunlight, the catering staff circulated with cups of coffee.

Blake and his team, along with Kaia and Royce began a delicate dance of shepherding everyone out the door while making sure they were entitled to any jewelry going out the door with them.

Tina had finally fallen asleep, off in the back room with Jo Jo, allowing for a thorough search of the party area. Other than a cufflink and a jeweled button, which could have been legitimately lost, they couldn't find anything else. Royce balanced his sales receipts and signed off on the inventory of remaining jewels. He and Kaia began dismantling the displays.

Blake and his team monitored the guests and retrieved their RFID tags as the valets quickly brought the cars around.

Fatigue suddenly hit Kaia and she sank onto the cushy chairs near Casper's office. She was tempted to stretch out, but was afraid she would fall asleep and miss Casper or his weasel. They had unfinished business that she hoped they could conclude before Blake wanted to leave.

She sat, head back, eyes closed, but opened them when she heard the office door. She expected to see Casper, but it was Tina sneaking out. She didn't notice Kaia sitting there.

I thought you were asleep.

Something about the way Tina walked gave Kaia a funny feeling.

She's got the snuffbox.

Kaia didn't know how she knew, but she did. She ran into the office and straight to the vase. The Cat's Eye was there, but the snuffbox wasn't.

"I hope this means good news," said a male voice and Casper entered by the French doors. "In anticipation of your success, I left your reward in the vase."

"You missed your wife by about three minutes," Kaia told him.

"Ah, that was intentional," Casper said. "Since she believes I'm in London and is leaving shortly to join me there. It's required some creative scheduling on my part, but worth it, I hope. The box, please."

"You'd better send someone to intercept your wife, because I put the snuffbox here, as we agreed, but I suspect she came in and took it again."

Casper's face changed immediately into something very unpleasant. "How could you have let that happen!"

"Your wife is a kleptomaniac! Your security people and I have spent the entire night retrieving things she stole from the guests!"

"You told others?" His face was turning such a dark red, Kaia wondered if he would have a stroke.

"You're missing the point. I didn't have to tell anyone. They saw her."

"No." He shook his head. "I don't believe you. You're trying to embarrass me, to get back at me. It didn't work before and it won't work now."

The man had gone a little insane. Kaia couldn't even get angry with him. "Tina has got a real problem and you need to get her some help."

"I will not be talked to in that manner by the likes of you!"

"The likes of me? You mean a thief, like your wife?" Casper's face was nearly purple.

Kaia didn't want him croaking before he could clear her name. She softened her voice. "You can't keep covering for her. Too many people know."

"We had an agreement!" He strode across the room.

"And I fulfilled my part of it. I put it in the vase." Kaia refused to let him make her angry. "If you want the snuffbox back, you'll have to ask your wife for it."

Ignoring her, Casper grabbed the vase and upended it. The pendant dropped to the desk. "There is no snuffbox."

"Because your wife took it," she repeated.

"I have only your word that she did." And he left no doubt of his opinion of Kaia's trustworthiness.

"Fine." Kaia started for the door. "I'll go get it from her."

"No!"

"I'll be discreet," she said sarcastically.

"Stop!"

There was a tap on the door and Blake opened it. If he was surprised to see Casper, he didn't indicate it. "Excuse me, Kaia, is this part of Royce's collection?" In his hand was the snuffbox.

She didn't know how or why he had it, only that he did. She met his eyes. "Thank you," she said under her breath. Louder, she answered, "No, it's not. It must belong here." She turned and gently placed it on Casper's desk.

He stared at it, breathing deeply. When he didn't say anything, Kaia picked it up and placed it in the vase. "I have fulfilled our agreement."

Quietly, Casper withdrew the snuffbox. "Unfortunately, you failed to keep anyone else from knowing about the snuffbox." He looked past her shoulder and she knew Blake was still in the room.

Her mouth went dry. "There were extenuating circumstances. A blackout."

Casper sat at his desk. Unlocking the drawer where he'd kept the chocolate replica, he placed the box and the pendant inside and took out the faxed agreement Tyrone had him sign. "There is nothing in this contract about 'extenuating circumstances.'" He met her eyes with a dismissive gaze. "A good lawyer would have thought of that." He ripped the paper in two.

Kaia stood there, frozen. He was doing it again. He was going to cheat and lie and get away with it again.

"I'll ask you to leave now." Casper locked the drawer. "Mr. McCauley, was there something in particular you needed to speak to me about?"

Numbly, Kaia pushed past Blake and fumbled for her cell phone. Tyrone would help her. He *had* to help her.

She was outside the office punching in the number when Blake spoke, loud and clear. "My men are making some repairs to the upstairs windows."

"Was there storm damage?" Casper asked.

"Just some minor adjustments for security purposes. The system will be down for about twenty minutes. I'll remain on-site until we've finished testing and it's back online."

Blake was giving her carte blanche to the house. Without knowing what was going on between her and Casper, he trusted her.

Wow. He really did love her. Grinning so wide her lips hurt, Kaia stayed out of sight as Blake and Casper left the office. And then she got to work.

BLAKE WATCHED AS KAIA scarfed down a delicious three-egg omelet with ham and cheese and other fatty goodness. He knew it was delicious, because an identical one sat on the plate in front of him.

They were in a breakfast place about a mile from Casper's house. They hadn't discussed what had happened after Kaia left Casper's office and Blake hadn't asked. But he really hoped she'd tell him.

He'd overheard her talking with Casper and figured out that she'd had some sort of side deal with him. When Tina's name came up, Blake suspected she'd lifted one more thing. Rather than confront her directly, he shamelessly used a snarling Jo Jo. "I can take that for you," he'd offered and took the box from her as he thrust the dog into her arms. Distracted by Jo Jo, Tina hadn't noticed when Blake pocketed the jeweled box instead of setting it on a table.

He didn't know what the thing was, but he knew Kaia needed it. Afterward, he heard enough to realize Casper was reneging on another deal.

"You haven't asked what I did," she said. Eyeing him over her orange juice, she took a long drink.

"I wanted you to tell me."

"I wanted to tell you. And I was going to, but afterward in my moment of triumph, not after getting taken by Casper again."

"You had a side deal with him. I've guessed that much."

Kaia nodded as the server refilled their coffee. "The snuffbox belongs to the Lithuanian embassy and Tina stole it during a dinner. Our government is investigating the guests. Casper was afraid Tina had it and even if she didn't, he was afraid her kleptomania would come out." She took a sip of coffee. "The deal was that if I recovered it without anyone knowing, he would clear my name."

"Kaia!"

She nodded. "He'd also give me back the Cat's Eye, but the real biggie was recanting his accusations."

"He'd be admitting to perjury." And Blake didn't see that happening.

"Alvin, the weasel—his lawyer—would have worked out something."

Blake rubbed at the condensation on his orange juice glass. "Kaia, I don't think so. You were set up from the beginning."

Shaking her head, she set her coffee mug back on the table. "I have a great lawyer."

"I mean, before." Blake had been thinking about it. "There had been a rash of thefts, but the Nazarios hadn't been hit until you. If anyone had any suspicions of Tina, they went away once you were arrested—and admitted to being in their houses. Think about it—there were five or however many opportunities for you to be caught. And when you weren't, Casper set you up and made Tina and him look like victims, too."

"Oh, my God." She stared at him. "You're right and I never saw it. He was trying to set me up last night, too. He left the pendant in the vase where I'd find it. But it was part of the deal. I have it in writing."

"Witnessed?"

She nodded. "Tyrone, my lawyer, was on the phone. He negotiated the agreement."

"And Casper's lawyer?"

"Wasn't there." She grimaced and squeezed her eyes shut. "Casper could claim extortion or something, right?"

"Probably." Blake was done with Casper. Once he

severed ties, he still had friends on the force. If he had to, he'd drop a few hints about Tina. "So let's see it."

She opened her eyes. "What?"

"The infamous Cat's Eye diamond."

"I don't have it." She picked up her fork and continued eating her omelet.

"I—I gave you twenty minutes! I figured that was more than enough time!"

"And I love you for that." She smiled. "'Course I love you without that, too."

"Yeah?" A grin spread across his face. She seemed okay and if she was okay, he was okay. "Kaia, I want you to know that your record doesn't affect my feelings for you. I'm sorry you went to prison and I'm sorry for my part in it. Someday, Casper will trip up. I have to believe that."

She activated her cell-phone screen. "It's been about forty-five minutes. I figure he'll be tripping soon."

"What do you mean?"

"You didn't ask me what I did with the twenty minutes you gave me." She took a biscuit and slathered butter on it.

"You're killing me here. What did you do?"

She looked pleased with herself. "Since our agreement was 'null and void', I put the snuffbox back."

"Back where?"

"In Tina's safe where I found it. If Casper wants the snuffbox, he'll have to ask her for it." She took a bite of the biscuit.

"Wait—hasn't Tina already left for London?"

Kaia nodded. "Oh, yes. Private helicopter. Lot of noise. And when we left, I believe the weasel was en route to pick up the snuffbox prior to his meeting with embassy officials."

Blake laughed. "That's brilliant! Now I get why you wanted to stop here for breakfast." Blake speared a mouthful of omelet. He'd better eat. They were going to be returning to Casper's soon.

"I was hungry! This is good. I don't normally eat butter or bread. Yum!" She was so calm.

"What do you think he'll do?" Blake was the one with the nerves.

"Call and threaten me." And right then, her phone buzzed. She looked at it on the table. "Shall I put it on speaker?"

"By all means." He held up a finger for her to wait, took out his phone and started recording.

She pressed the screen. "Kaia Bennet."

"Where is it?" erupted Casper's voice.

"Where is what?"

"You know exactly what I'm talking about."

"I'm not a mind reader."

A couple of beats went by and Blake figured Casper knew he was going on the record, but wasn't in a position to make demands.

"Where did you put the snuffbox?" Casper enunciated clearly.

Be careful, Blake mouthed at her.

"Once you voided our agreement, everything reverted to its prior state," Kaia said.

Not bad, Blake thought.

"Ms. Bennet," sounded another voice Blake recognized as Casper's lawyer. "We would like to negotiate another agreement with you."

"You have my lawyer's number," Kaia told him. "He's expecting your call." She disconnected.

"What do you think will happen?" Blake asked her.

"I think we'll have to finish our breakfast quickly

so we can head back to Casper's. I'm in a very good negotiating position, thanks to you."

Blake shook his head. "You did this all by yourself. I just gave you the opportunity."

"Let's talk about that. You trusted me to do the right thing. Even better, you trusted me to figure out the right thing." She grinned. "You can tell me you love me now."

He started to do just that, but something prompted him to say instead, "I trust you."

Kaia's expression changed from happy to luminous. "Blake," she whispered, her eyes bright.

Were those tears? He reached for her hand across the table. "I need you to trust me, too. I want to start fresh with you and I need you to trust me not to mess it up this time. Can you?"

When she stayed silent, he added, "I love you. I never stopped."

She covered their clasped hands with her other one. "You hurt me a lot."

"I know."

Drawing a deep breath, she said, "I forgive you, I do, but I can't forget what that felt like. Not yet."

"I understand." He hadn't forgotten what it felt like, either. "Maybe we're not supposed to forget. Maybe remembering will remind us to be honest with each other."

"And not to take each other for granted," she said.

"Yeah. I like that. This is going to work, isn't it?"

"Absolutely," Blake said, beyond grateful that he was getting a second chance from a woman who didn't believe in second chances.

They smiled at each other and slowly unclasped their hands.

"And one more thing," Blake said as Kaia reached for her coffee.

"What?"

He held up his bare wrist. "Give me back my watch."

* * * * *

COMING NEXT MONTH

Blaze's 10th Anniversary
Special Collectors' Editions

Available July 26, 2011

#627 THE BRADDOCK BOYS: TRAVIS
Love at First Bite
Kimberly Raye

#628 HOTSHOT
Uniformly Hot!
Jo Leigh

#629 UNDENIABLE PLEASURES
The Pleasure Seekers
Tori Carrington

#630 COWBOYS LIKE US
Sons of Chance
Vicki Lewis Thompson

#631 TOO HOT TO TOUCH
Legendary Lovers
Julie Leto

#632 EXTRA INNINGS
Encounters
Debbi Rawlins

HBCNM0711

REQUEST YOUR FREE BOOKS!
2 FREE NOVELS PLUS 2 FREE GIFTS!

red-hot reads!

*Once bitten, twice shy. That's Gabby Wade's motto—
especially when it comes to Adamson men.
And the moment she meets Jon Adamson her theory
is confirmed. But with each encounter a little something
sparks between them, making her wonder if she's been
too hasty to dismiss this one!*

*Enjoy this sneak peek from ONE GOOD REASON
by Sarah Mayberry, available August 2011
from Harlequin® Superromance®.*

Gabby Wade's heartbeat thumped in her ears as she marched to her office. She wanted to pretend it was because of her brisk pace returning from the file room, but she wasn't that good a liar.

Her heart was beating like a tom-tom because Jon Adamson had touched her. In a very male, very possessive way. She could still feel the heat of his big hand burning through the seat of her khakis as he'd steadied her on the ladder.

It had taken every ounce of self-control to tell him to unhand her. What she'd really wanted was to grab him by his shirt and, well, explore all those urges his touch had instantly brought to life.

While she might not like him, she was wise enough to understand that it wasn't always about liking the other person. Sometimes it was about pure animal attraction.

Refusing to think about it, she turned to work. When she'd typed in the wrong figures three times, Gabby admitted she was too tired and too distracted. Time to call it a day.

As she was leaving, she spied Jon at his workbench in the shop. His head was propped on his hand as he studied blueprints. It wasn't until she got closer that she saw his eyes were shut.

He looked oddly boyish. There was something innocent and unguarded in his expression. She felt a weakening in her resistance to him.

"Jon." She put her hand on his shoulder, intending to shake him awake. Instead, it rested there like a caress.

His eyes snapped open.

"You were asleep."

"No, I was, uh, visualizing something on this design." He gestured to the blueprint in front of him then rubbed his eyes.

That gesture dealt a bigger blow to her resistance. She realized it wasn't only animal attraction pulling them together. She took a step backward as if to get away from the knowledge.

She cleared her throat. "I'm heading off now."

He gave her a smile, and she could see his exhaustion.

"Yeah, I should, too." He stood and stretched. The hem of his T-shirt rose as he arched his back and she caught a flash of hard male belly. She looked away, but it was too late. Her mind had committed the image to permanent memory.

And suddenly she knew, for good or bad, she'd never look at Jon the same way again.

Find out what happens next in ONE GOOD REASON, available August 2011 from Harlequin® Superromance®!

Celebrating

Blaze 10 *years of*

red-hot reads

Featuring a special August author lineup of
six fan-favorite authors who have written
for Blaze™ from the beginning!

The Original Sexy Six:

Vicki Lewis Thompson
Tori Carrington
Kimberly Raye
Debbi Rawlins
Julie Leto
Jo Leigh

Pick up all six Blaze™
Special Collectors' Edition titles!

August 2011

USA TODAY *bestselling author*

Lynne Graham

introduces her new Epic Duet

THE VOLAKIS VOW
A marriage made of secrets…

Tally Spencer, an ordinary girl with no experience of relationships… Sander Volakis, an impossibly rich and handsome Greek entrepreneur. Sander is expecting to love her and leave her, but for Tally this is love at first sight. Little does he know that Tally is expecting his baby…and blackmailing him to marry her!

PART ONE:
THE MARRIAGE BETRAYAL
Available August 2011

PART TWO:
BRIDE FOR REAL
Available September 2011

Available only from Harlequin Presents®.

HP13005